"And just what is it that you really want to do—but don't?" Leonor asked him in a voice that had mysteriously gone down to just above a whisper.

As it was, her voice sounded very close to husky—and he found it hopelessly seductive.

Standing just inside her suite, Leonor waited for him to answer while her heart continued to imitate the rhythm of a drum roll that only grew louder by the moment.

Josh weighed his options for a moment. Damned if he did and damned if he didn't, he couldn't help thinking. And then he answered her.

"Kiss you," he told Leonor, saying the words softly, his breath caressing the skin on her face.

She felt her stomach muscles quickening.

"Maybe you should go ahead and do that," she told him. "I promise I won't stop you."

* * *

The Coltons of Shadow Creek:
Only family can keep you safe…

COLTON UNDERCOVER

BY
MARIE FERRARELLA

This is a work of fiction. Names, characters, places, locations and incidents are purely fictional and bear no relationship to any real life individuals, living or dead, or to any actual places, business establishments, locations, events or incidents. Any resemblance is entirely coincidental.

First Published in Great Britain 2017
By Mills & Boon, an imprint of HarperCollins*Publishers*
1 London Bridge Street, London, SE1 9GF

Special thanks and acknowledgement are given to Marie Ferrarella for her contribution to *The Coltons of Shadow Creek* series.

ISBN: 978-0-263-93036-8

18-0417

Our policy i
products an
manufacturi
the country

Printed and
by CPI, Bar

USA TODAY bestselling and RITA® Award-winning author **Marie Ferrarella** has written more than two-hundred-and-fifty books for Mills & Boon, some under the name Marie Nicole. Her romances are beloved by fans worldwide. Visit her website, www.marieferrarella.com.

To
Patience Bloom
Who Seems To Have
Enough Faith In Me
To Believe I Can
Pull Off Yet Another
Continuity.
Thank You!

Prologue

"You, lady, are a real piece of work."

At the moment, there was no one else in the FBI field office in San Antonio, Texas with Special Agent Joshua Howard. His words were addressed to the photograph of Livia Colton he had pulled from the file on his desk. A file he had gone over and reviewed countless times in the last few days.

Livia, or rather, her untimely escape from prison, was the reason he was about to temporarily relocate to Shadow Creek, a place unofficially known as "the town that Livia built," and with good reason.

Josh shook his head as by now all too familiar details danced before his brown eyes. The life of the attractive, blond-haired, fifty-two-year-old illegitimate product of a one-night stand between one of the wealthier Coltons and a drug-addicted prostitute read like something out of a Hollywood movie, right down to the part where, by all indications, Livia's once-unchecked sociopathic behavior rivaled that of a classic "bad seed."

While behaving lovingly toward her easily manipulated father, Livia was ruthless toward her half siblings. Rumor had it that, by his own admission, Livia was the only person whom Matthew Colton, her convicted serial killer half brother, truly feared. In Josh's book, that was saying a great deal.

Marrying and discarding husbands as if they were used tissues, Livia amassed a considerable fortune and six children along the way, all presumably with different fathers. Resorting to her natural cunning, she managed to quadruple her fortune through organized crime. She'd trafficked in drugs, women and whatever else might have been profitable at the moment.

Her children, she barely tolerated unless there was a photographer within the vicinity to immortalize her with them. She had been a great one for photo ops. There had been one offspring, her oldest daughter, Leonor, whom people said she disliked less than the rest.

Not exactly a glowing testimony, Josh thought.

The living definition of a wild child Livia Colton had finally given, before her downfall, at least outwardly, all the signs of wanting to settle down. She'd gotten married again, this time to an Argentine horse breeder who it was said treated her children far better than she did. She had had her last child, Jade, with him.

Playing the part of a benevolent pillar of the community, Livia built the town she had adopted a much-needed hospital, funded most of their 4-H program, allowed other ranchers to use her water supply without charge and threw legendary parties. Shadow Creek's society worshipfully revolved around her. No one questioned where her rather fabulous wealth came from, especially not those who benefited from it.

But eventually, the law, steadily collecting evidence against her over the years, managed to bring charges against Livia. Ten years ago the onetime queen of Shadow Creek was convicted of numerous charges, including murder. She had just barely avoided the death penalty—*bribing the judge no doubt,* Josh thought—and was sentenced to serve five life sentences in Red Peak Maximum Security Prison in Gatesville, Texas. Her neighbors all turned their backs on her, her vast fortune was confiscated and her six children were left to fend for themselves the best way that they could.

It sounded, Josh thought, like a perfect ending, with justice being served—except that, maximum security prison or not, Livia had managed to escape two weeks ago. The first thought that occurred to him was that one of her children must have been instrumental in bringing about her escape and was currently helping and sheltering her.

But which one?

He'd looked into all their backgrounds.

Josh spread out the six assorted photographs, some candid, some professional, of Livia's children.

They were nothing if not an eclectic bunch, he thought. They only had one thing in common—well, two, if he counted that they all had the same mother—or at least that was what the birth certificates said. Claudia, her second youngest, had been born while she was traveling in Europe and there was only Livia's word that she'd given birth to the girl.

Each of her children was good-looking in his or her own way. It was always harder confronting attractive people and getting them to confess, Josh mused. Somehow, they thought that their looks would help shield them from the dire consequences of their actions: in essence, their "get-out-of-jail-for-free" cards.

But he intended to confront them, because one—if not more—of them was responsible for Livia's escape.

Finding out who it was, how they had engineered it and where they—and Livia—currently were was the job he'd been assigned by the Bureau. And it was why he had his "go bag" stashed in the trunk of his silver sedan. He was leaving for Shadow Creek.

Apparently all the siblings, except for River, Livia's third born, were finding their way home after having scattered once Livia's trial was over.

Of the six, his gut was pointing him toward Leonor Colton. Out of all of Livia's children, Leonor was the only one who visited Livia while she was in prison. He knew that Leonor certainly had the money to finance her mother's escape. He'd just conducted a check on her accounts and saw that there had been a large withdrawal made a few months ago.

Was that money used to bribe guards to look the other way?

And there was more. Leonor had just recently returned "home" to Shadow Creek and Josh had to wonder why. Was it to reconnect with her roots, or just with her mother? Granted, by all accounts, Livia Colton made Joan Crawford come across like Mother of the Year in comparison, but desperate times meant desperate measures and if the woman was to turn to any of her six children, it would be Leonor.

Livia had already been sighted once in these last two weeks, around the time when the man who had kidnapped her grandson, Cody, was killed. Josh had a strong feeling that the woman had been involved and was responsible, at least indirectly, for the man's death.

That meant that she was somewhere in the state. Maybe even close by.

Working on this assumption, Josh got ready to go.

"Next stop," he murmured under his breath, his voice echoing about the empty office, "Shadow Creek. Hopefully to slap the cuffs on you, Livia—and whoever it is that's been helping you. Playtime," he informed the woman's photograph just before closing the file and putting it into his folder, "is over. It's time for you to pay the piper."

Smiling grimly, Josh left the office.

Chapter 1

Thanks to the special trust fund her late father had set up for her, unlike many people her age, thirty-one-year-old Leonor Colton didn't need to work. She *wanted* to work. Wanted to put her art degree to use and do something that made her feel as if she was contributing in some small way to society. That was why she had initially taken that unpaid internship at the Austin Art Museum. While others might have floated along, especially since they weren't getting paid, Leonor worked exceptionally hard. She put in long hours, coming in early and staying late, long after the museum had been closed to the public.

All this hard work managed to impress Adam Sheffield, the director who was in charge of the museum, so much so that once her internship was over, he offered her the job of assistant curator. She took it gladly and worked her way up to her current position of curator.

For a while, Leonor thought, looking back now, things had seemed as if they were going quite well for her. Better than well. She had managed to hold her head high, despite the devastating scandal that had all but ripped her family apart. Because of her mother's arrest and subsequent conviction—something that neither she nor any of her siblings saw coming—they had gone from being at the pinnacle of Shadow Creek's community to being objects of everyone else's contempt.

Leonor had risen above the gossip and mean-spirited talk, ignoring it and going on with her life. She'd gotten her education—a degree in the arts—and a job she loved in her chosen field. Even her love life had taken a much-needed turn for the better.

Or so she had thought.

Up until that point, the redheaded, green-eyed Leonor had only dated sporadically and she had never had a serious relationship—possibly because of the love 'em and leave 'em example that her mother had set for all of them.

And then David Marshall had come along.

Handsome, charming and oh-so-smooth, David had completely swept her off her feet in what amounted to record time. Looking back, Leonor couldn't believe how quickly she'd surrendered to him, taking down her barriers and opening up her heart. She must have been crazy. But from the bottom of that isolated heart, she had honestly believed that David Marshall was the man she was meant to marry.

Desperately needing to have someone to talk to and trust, in a short amount of time Leonor had completely opened herself up to him and told David not just who she was, but also made him privy to all of her family's numerous and heretofore well-kept secrets.

It felt so wonderful to finally open up to someone, to have someone she could really talk to without being afraid of any sort of censorship or being looked down upon judgmentally.

She should have been afraid, Leonor thought ruefully now. Considering everything she had been through with her mother's arrest, she should have been leery, not trusting.

Water under the bridge, she thought regretfully.

A few months ago, after things seemed to be going so well, she woke up one morning to find that David was not only gone from her bed, but gone, it soon became apparent, from her life, as well. And not long after that she found out that he had not only stolen her heart, but he'd taken a very large chunk of her money with him as well. No note, no explanation, not even an argument to serve as a foreshadowing of things to come.

He had just vanished without any warning.

It wasn't the money she missed. Because of the way the trust fund had been set up, there was more than enough money left, money that David hadn't been able to get his hands on. But she wasn't angry about that. She was angry, hurt and confused because he had left her for no good reason.

Or so she thought.

But everything fell into place when one day she'd opened up her computer, logged onto the internet and saw that her family's story was splashed all over the home page of Everything's Blogger in Texas, a local gossip site.

Reading the first installment—she couldn't pull her eyes away—Leonor felt like such a fool.

She still felt that way. All those things David had said to her—he had just been playing her, lying to her so that she would trust him and learn to confide in him, telling him all of her family's secrets. Secrets he then turned around and sold to the blog.

Leonor felt incredibly stupid and used. And horribly crushed.

In its own way, this was as devastating to her as her mother's arrest had been that awful, awful day over ten years ago when the law enforcement officers had descended on the sprawling mansion that she and her brothers and sisters called home.

At first, after David's disappearance and bitter betrayal, she had sought refuge in her position at the museum. But it didn't help her keep her mind off what a fool she had been. So she'd gone to her boss and asked Sheffield for a leave of absence in the hopes that if she went somewhere else, she'd be able to somehow pull herself together.

"I'm not losing you, am I, Leonor?" Adam Sheffield had asked, concerned as he sat with her in his office, looking at her across his cluttered desk. "Because, I don't mind telling you, in all my years here, you're the best curator I've ever had." He'd leaned forward, lowering his voice and creating an air of privacy. "If it's a matter of more money—"

She'd been quick to shoot that supposition down. "No, it's not that, Mr. Sheffield. I don't want more money."

"Shorter hours, then," he proposed, guessing at the reason behind her unanticipated request. "I know I've been relying on you a great deal—maybe too much—but you're so damn good at this that—"

She'd stopped the director mid-sentence again. "Thank you, sir, but it's not the hours, either, Mr. Sheffield." Leonor went on to appeal to his kinder side. "I just need to get away for a while, pull myself together. I haven't seen my family for a long time and I think it might be time to go back home for a little while."

"But not permanently." It was more of a request than a question. He'd looked at her nervously, obviously afraid of the answer he might get.

"No, not permanently," Leonor replied.

In all honesty, she didn't know if she wouldn't just turn around and return to Austin after a few days in Shadow Creek. She didn't know how welcome—or unwelcome—she'd be turning up in Shadow Creek after all this time and in the wake of that lurid blog exposé.

Oh, she knew that she could stay at Mac's ranch, perhaps even indefinitely. Her former stepfather, Joseph Mackenzie, her mother's former ranch foreman as well as the father of her half brother, Thorne, had made that perfectly clear, even before she had used some of her money to help him bail out his ranch a few years ago.

Mac had always had a special relationship with all of her mother's children, not just with her or with his own son. Mac was a kind, decent person and the kind of man she would have really loved to have for a father, even temporarily, as was her mother's habit.

He'd always been there for them, Leonor recalled. And he was the first one she thought of calling on when she found herself needing a place to stay while she regrouped.

"Of course you can stay here, little girl," Mac had told her when she'd turned up on his doorstep. "Stay for as long as you want. My home is your home. Hell, it wouldn't even *be* my home if it hadn't been for you," he reminded her.

He'd displayed no embarrassment over that admission, only extreme gratitude.

Mac picked up her suitcase as he talked, doing it effortlessly as if finding her there when he opened his front door was no big deal.

"Oh, Mac," she cried as he put his large, still-muscular arm protectively about her shoulders and ushered her in, "I've made such a mess of things."

There was nothing but sympathy in his eyes and in his manner toward her.

Even though she was going to be staying in the apartment over the stable, Mac led Livia's daughter to the wide leather sofa in his living room and sat her down. Seeing the tears in her eyes, he pulled out his handkerchief from his back pocket and offered it to her.

"There's nothing but death that can't be undone," he told Leonor matter-of-factly. "You didn't kill anyone, did you?"

"No," she'd said, quietly sobbing.

She wiped away her tears, but it was futile. More tears came to take their place. She felt as if she was completely made up of water.

"Then it can be fixed," Mac had assured her. Studying her face quietly, he'd asked, "Do you want to talk about it?"

At first, Leonor had remained silent.

Mac wasn't the kind of person to press.

But then, after a few minutes, he'd heard her say, "I trusted the wrong man."

"Hardly anyone alive hasn't done that at least once in their lives," Mac told her, making it sound like a common occurrence. After a beat, Mac ventured a question. "How bad is it?"

She pressed her lips together in an effort to keep a fresh onslaught of tears back. "Bad," she'd finally answered.

He'd smiled at her kindly. He had always viewed her first and foremost as a daughter, even if they didn't share the same blood.

"Would it help any if I tracked this guy down and beat the living daylights out of him?"

"No." She thought about the blog. The story, done

in several vivid, lurid installments, had already been run. The rest of her siblings had probably already seen it. And probably hated her for it. Only traveling back in time could change that. "The damage has already been done."

"Oh," Mac had said. His deep voice rumbled out the single word, putting a huge amount of meaning behind it. "You're talking about that internet story, aren't you?"

Leonor's eyes had widened as she looked at the man who had patiently taught her how to ride. The man she had always regarded as more than just her mother's foreman, or even Thorne's father. He had always been the single stable force in her life.

Had she disappointed him?

"You saw that?" she asked in a small, ashamed voice.

Mac had surprised her by laughing. "I'm not quite as backward as you might think. I own a laptop and sometimes, I even turn it on."

Leonor flushed. "I didn't mean to insult you—"

His smile was wide and all encompassing, as well as very kind. "You didn't, little girl. I'm just teasing you. But I did see the articles," he said, referring to the tell-all that went into great detail about not just Livia before her empire had crumbled and she'd been sent to prison, but also about each of the woman's six children and their lives, "and I thought to myself that whoever wrote it had to have a lot of inside information about the Coltons from someone." The look on his face registered surprise, but not condemnation. "I just never thought that the 'someone' was you."

She was desperate to make Mac understand that she hadn't revealed any of it for personal gain or, heaven forbid, for any sort of monetary reward. "He tricked me, Mac. He made me think that he cared about me. I would have never said a single word if I'd known that he was going to use it to spread it all over the internet."

Mac nodded understandingly. "I kinda figured that," he told her.

There was absolutely not a single iota of judgment in the man's deep voice.

Leonor pressed her lips together, and then raised her tear-filled eyes to his. "I thought he loved me," she confessed, her voice almost trembling. "I thought I could tell him anything. He *told* me I could tell him anything."

"I just bet he did," Mac replied, doing his best to keep his anger in check. "You sure you don't want me to track him down and beat him up for you?" This time, as Mac clenched his hands into fists beside him on the sofa, he was only half kidding.

"I don't want you getting into trouble on my account," Leonor told him.

"Might do us both some good," he pointed out, coaxing her just the tiniest bit.

Leonor looked up at him quizzically. She knew why he thought it would do her some good, but Mac? She didn't quite understand why he would say that.

"Why you?"

"Because I don't like anyone hurting you," he told her simply.

She felt her heart swell. She really needed to hear that, she thought.

"Thank you, Mac." She returned his smile, wondering how she could possibly convey to the man how grateful she was to have him in her life. "Letting me stay here for a while is all I need."

She sighed and put her arms around Mac—or tried to. There was more of the big man than her arms could possibly encompass.

Mac laughed softly—she'd always thought of his laugh as such a comforting sound—and embraced her.

"Like I said, stay as long as you like. I want you to think of this as your home," he told her again without any fanfare.

That had been four days ago. So, here she was, Leonor thought, hiding out at Mac's ranch, doing her best to pull herself together and regroup enough to be able to face each of her siblings, preferably individually, so she could field their questions and get them to hear her out and see her side.

She needed to have them forgive her, if not today, then eventually. Forgive her and see that she was as much of a victim in all this as they were, because they might be resentful to see their names and their lives shockingly dramatized online in a cheap effort at sensationalism. But David had used her to do this to them and she was not only suffering the same fate as they were, she was also suffering because someone she loved and believed loved her had done this, using her as a means to an end. And in the bargain, making her family look at her as a traitor. She'd reported him to the police, but he had hidden the money well and it was a case of her word against his. Things looked rather bleak from every standpoint.

She had trouble battling the hopelessness that kept insisting on encroaching on her state of mind. But if she hoped to ever win back her family, she had to keep that feeling at bay.

Well, this was unexpected, Josh thought, checking his email the moment he checked into the bed and breakfast when he arrived in Shadow Creek.

Leonor Colton had taken a leave of absence from the museum.

Josh frowned. He had gone undercover, taking on the identity of a billionaire with a keen interest in art and the museum, in order to become a person of interest to Leonor so that he could get closer to her, and now she'd taken a leave of absence. Josh shook his head. This was going to be trickier than he thought.

Well, it was too late to switch identities again because in this day and age everyone's "backstory" could be checked out on the internet in a matter of minutes, and his was already a matter of record. That was thanks to Jeremy Bailey, the IT wizard in the San Antonio field office who had whipped up this identity for him. Jeremy had even created a Facebook page for him, cleverly backdated with photographs of an ex-wife and a number of parties and fund-raisers—all art-oriented—that he'd attended in the past.

Josh pulled up the page on his laptop now, wondering who the woman posing as his ex-wife was. Whoever Jeremy had used, the woman was a little too flashy for him, he mused. He preferred more classy women, women whose brains were stuffed to full capacity instead of just their closets.

So far, Josh hadn't met anyone who could hold his interest for more than a few dates, but then, in defense of all the women he had ever gone out with, he'd never had the time to properly pursue a relationship.

For one thing, he had moved around a lot, transferring to different field offices whenever new opportunities arose. Single, with no family, he had nothing to keep him anchored to any one place.

With him, it was always the next case that piqued his interest.

But at the moment, it wasn't the next one that did it. It was *this* one.

He had set his sights on bringing Livia Colton in, and to do that, he had already decided that he was going to have to get close to Leonor. Some of the circumstances might have changed, but the bottom line was still the same.

He just needed to do a little rewriting to make it ultimately work and he was nothing, he thought, smiling to himself, if not creatively flexible.

"You're going down, Livia Colton," he promised. "And so's your daughter if she's in on this."

He got to work.

Chapter 2

"Just remember, you don't have access to a bottomless expense account." Andrew Arroyo's voice crackled a little, thanks to a poor cell phone connection. "The budget's been cut, so be sure you watch how you throw that money around, Howard," the FBI assistant director in charge of the San Antonio field office warned him. "Just because you're supposed to be this big shot billionaire doesn't mean you have to spend money like one. As a matter of fact," Arroyo hinted helpfully, "a lot of billionaires are known to be tight when it comes to their money."

Josh was beginning to regret checking in with his superior so soon after arriving in Shadow Creek. He should have waited until he had something a little more solid by way of an alternate plan to offer the man.

Still, Josh felt he needed to say something defensively before he found his hands completely tied in this little undercover drama he'd found himself taking part in.

"I can't exactly penny-pinch, Assistant Director Arroyo," Josh told his boss matter-of-factly. "I *am* supposed to be a billionaire."

"The operative word here being 'supposed to be,'" Arroyo pointed out.

If he'd really liked Arroyo, he would have just kept quiet about this lecture. But he didn't. Arroyo liked to micromanage everyone assigned to him and that wasn't the way that Josh liked to operate.

"That's three words, sir," Josh replied matter-of-factly.

He could almost *hear* Arroyo scowling. The assistant director had the kind of scowl that took in every single part of his face. "Don't nitpick, Howard."

"I won't if you won't, sir," Josh responded. And then he grew serious as he tried to explain his position. It was the only plan he could think of to make himself privy to Leonor's movements without arousing her suspicions. "It's a work in progress, but the plan is to have Leonor Colton try to get close to me so she can try to convince me to donate to the museum."

"You can play hard to get," Arroyo suggested. "Nothing makes a woman want a man more than if he acts as if he's not interested."

In his opinion, his superior would be the last person anyone would go to for advice on getting close to a member of the opposite sex.

"Which might explain why you've never been married," Josh observed under his breath.

"I heard that," Arroyo snapped. "We're not talking about me. We're talking about you and the Bureau's rather limited expense account."

Calling Arroyo had definitely been a mistake on his part, Josh thought. He was just going to have to work things out to his own satisfaction. "As stimulating as this conversation is, sir, I've got a plan to get into motion. I'll check in with you later," Josh promised vaguely.

Just before pigs begin to fly, he added silently.

The next minute, Josh terminated the call and put away his cell phone before his superior could protest or say anything else.

He was on his own, Josh thought, going back to the laptop he'd left open on the desk. Sitting down, he pulled up the site that had caught his eye. The one currently featuring the Everything's Blogger in Texas story about the individual members of Livia Colton's family.

It contained, he couldn't help thinking, an amazing amount of information, the kind that families generally liked being kept private. At least *some* of it had to be true, right?

He went on reading.

Leonor opened the studio apartment door in response to the knock she'd heard. Mac was standing on the landing just beyond the wooden stairs that went down to the back of the stable. He looked just a little larger than life—the way he always did. Stepping back to give him access to the apartment, she looked at him curiously.

"Something wrong?" she wanted to know.

Mac crossed the threshold, but made no attempt to come in any farther. If she were to make a guess, she would have said that he looked a little uncomfortable, which was unusual for the man.

"Don't take this the wrong way, little girl," he began, "because you know I care about you and I always have."

She didn't think she liked the sound of this, but Mac had never been anything but kind to her. "What are you trying to tell me, Mac?"

His kindly expression didn't match the words that came out of his mouth. "Get out."

Stunned, she could only stare at the tall, strapping man. "What?"

"I don't mean 'get out' get out," he told her, tempering his tone. He didn't want her to misunderstand what had motivated his words. "Just get out."

This was only getting more muddled. There wasn't much in her life that she was sure of these days, but she was sure that Mac wouldn't deliberately hurt her or abandon her.

Taking a breath, she asked, "And the difference being?"

He wasn't much for talking, more a man of deeds rather than words. He tried to make himself understood again.

"The difference being that you need to get out

there, little girl. Get out there and *mingle.* You can't just hide up here in this tiny space above the stable indefinitely. That's not going to solve anything and the longer you hide, the harder it's going to be for you to finally get out there." His eyes met hers, hoping he was getting through to her. "Thirty-one is way too young to become a hermit."

She sighed. Turning from him, she crossed back to the bed and sat down on the edge. "You're right."

Mac had no choice but to follow her in. "Of course I'm right. I've always been right.

"Well, almost always," Mac corrected. "The point is, little girl—go out. Breathe some fresh air. Get in touch with yourself again. There's a really nice person inside there," he told her. "You might like her. I know that I do."

She offered Mac a ghost of a smile. "You have to say that."

"No, I don't," he informed her. "That's not even in the fine print," he added affectionately. "Now get out of here before I hitch you up and use you to plow the north forty," he pretended to threaten.

Leonor laughed. She knew that, as usual, Mac only had her best interests at heart. And he was right. She couldn't just hide here in this little studio apartment forever. Eventually, she had to get back to her life. Getting up off the bed, she said, "I'm gone."

His brows drew together in a skeptical furrow. "I can still see you."

"Then close your eyes," she told him with a laugh.

"I need a head start." With that, Leonor left the apartment and hurried down the stairs.

Once in her car, Leonor drove into town. She decided to go get some lunch at the new restaurant that had just recently opened just across from the bed-and-breakfast.

Although she lived in Austin now, Leonor knew in her heart that Shadow Creek would always be home to her, and despite everything else that was going on in her life, she did take an interest in the town's development and growth, slow though it was.

Leonor tried to tell herself that checking out the new restaurant would be a fun thing to do. Most of the people in the area, while not completely forgetting about her mother and the scandal attached to both Livia's arrest and her trial, had for the most part moved on. At the very least, most of the locals had come to realize that the sins of the mother did not always necessarily come down on the offspring.

The town seemed to finally be coming around to the fact that none of them were anything like their mother.

Heaven knew that she certainly wasn't, even though she had gone to visit her mother several times in prison. That was more out of a sense of filial obligation, more because she felt sorry for her mother than anything else. Everyone else in the family had abandoned Livia and turned their backs on her.

Leonor supposed that she was the most sensitive one in the family.

However, being sensitive didn't mean that she was a pushover, she told herself fiercely, although there were some who undoubtedly thought she was.

Even so, she had to give herself a pep talk before she entered the restaurant. Because she was the daughter of the "notorious" Livia Colton and because she hadn't really been around these last ten years, she knew there would be those who would be looking at her with unspoken curiosity. She had to remind herself that she wasn't that awkward, gawky girl whose body had taken its sweet time before all the parts were in equal proportion.

She was who she was, Leonor reminded herself, and she had to own that no matter what. If being Livia Colton's daughter made other people uncomfortable, that was their problem, not hers. People didn't get to choose their family.

Now all she had to do was *believe* that, Leonor thought ruefully.

Happily, the restaurant, while doing a nice, brisk business, wasn't crowded in the big city sense of the word. The restaurants she had gotten accustomed to in Austin were the kind that had lines curling outside the door even *with* reservations. Waiting was more or less a way of life in Austin.

That wasn't the case here.

"Table for two, Ms. Colton?" the hostess asked as Leonor came up to the reservations desk.

Leonor was surprised that the hostess knew who she was. But she knew she shouldn't have been.

* * *

Standing not too far away, Josh heard someone being addressed as "Ms. Colton." He looked up sharply.

It was her.

Leonor Colton. She looked just like her picture. *Talk about luck*, he thought. He'd just stopped to get something to eat and he'd struck the mother lode.

As unobtrusively as possible, Josh made his way over to the reservations desk, trying not to appear to be in any sort of hurry.

Leonor's eyes met the hostess's. The latter appeared to be friendly. There was no condemnation or curiosity in the young woman's eyes. Leonor relaxed.

"No, just for one. I'm dining alone," Leonor told the hostess.

"You know," a deep voice directly behind her said, "I really hate dining alone, but I'm new in town so I suppose that I'll have to. Unless, perhaps, you wouldn't mind sharing a table with me."

"I'm sorry," Leonor replied without bothering to turn around. "I don't eat with strangers."

Rather than pretending to be put off, Josh circled around her until he was right in her line of vision. The hostess, who was looking on, seemed utterly charmed by him. But his target was not the hostess: it was Leonor Colton.

"My name's Joshua Pendergrass. Now, if you tell me your name, we won't be strangers anymore." He put out his hand, but Leonor made no effort to take it. Her hand remained at her side.

"Look, Mr. Pendergrass," she began patiently, "knowing your name doesn't make you any less of a stranger to me." She didn't want to cause a scene, but she really wanted the man to go away or at least back off. Granted, he was exceedingly handsome, but so was David, and look where that had gotten her. "I don't know the first thing about you."

Unfazed, Josh began to give her a thumbnail version of the bio that had been drawn up for him in the field office. "Easily taken care of. My father's Elliott Pendergrass and he and his firm have built some of the tallest buildings in Dallas and Austin. Much to my socialite mother's delight, my father loves finding new ways to build up the family fortune."

Leaning in just a shade closer to Leonor, he confided in a slightly lower tone, "He's on record as being very disappointed in me because my interests lie in a totally different field. I'm an art aficionado, and for me heaven is either spending the day prowling about the halls of an art museum, or just sitting in my den, admiring my own rather small, but if I do say so myself, modestly impressive collection. There," he concluded, flashing a rather world-class smile at her that caused the hostess behind her to sigh just a little, "will that do?"

Leonor didn't know whether to be amazed—or suspicious. David had done that to her, she thought angrily; he'd made her suspicious of things she would have once happily accepted at face value. He'd robbed her of her ability to be outgoing and friendly.

Still, after what this man with the incredible smile had just thrown out there, she had to ask. "You're an art lover?"

The man who had asked to share a table with her laughed softly at her question. "I'm afraid it's much more serious than that. It's more like I'm obsessed with art. At least that's the way my father puts it. He had really high hopes of getting me to follow him into the business." The wide shoulders beneath the expensive jacket rose and fell in a careless shrug. "I'm afraid I don't have a head for business. I do, however, know what I like, and I really like art."

"What kind of art?" Leonor challenged. She wanted to believe this was some sort of happy cosmic coincidence, but she'd learned the hard way that she needed to be cautious. "Abstract, modern, contemporary—?"

"A little bit of everything." When suspicion creased her brow, he confessed frankly, "I'm rather eclectic. Tell you what, why don't we continue this conversation over lunch?" he suggested. Looking over his shoulder, Josh nodded at the person behind him. "I'm afraid there's a line beginning to form behind us and this lovely young woman—Kathy," he said, reading the hostess's name tag, "is just too polite to move us along. I wouldn't want her getting into trouble on our account. Table for two, please, Kathy."

"Wait, I haven't agreed to share a table with you

yet," Leonor protested, holding up her hand to the hostess to keep her from leading them into the dining area.

Josh looked at her soulfully. "Would you deny a visitor to your town a little friendly conversation over lunch?"

"How do you know I'm not a visitor, too?" Leonor wanted to know, although she had to admit that some of her resistance was fading.

Josh's expression was nothing if not innocent. It was a look he practiced in the mirror from time to time to make sure he could still pull off.

"Are you?" he asked her.

"Not in the strictest sense, no," Leonor was forced to admit.

Rather than challenge her ambiguous statement, Josh raised one eyebrow in a silent question as he looked at her. And then he repeated, "Table for two?"

Leonor relented. What was the harm? After all, they'd be out in the open and she was free to leave at any given moment if she wanted to. So, nodding, she looked at the hostess and echoed his words.

"Table for two."

"Right this way," the hostess responded, leading them into the heart of the dining room. She took them to a secluded table that was off to one side. "I thought you might prefer this."

Leonor flashed a grateful smile at the hostess for what she assumed was the woman's kindness. "Thank you."

The hostess nodded in response. "Someone will

be back for your order," she told them as she placed two menus on the table before them, and then discreetly withdrew, saying, "Take your time."

"And enjoy your lunch," she added just before she slipped away.

"Your father really builds skyscrapers?" Leonor asked the moment the hostess had retreated back to the reservations desk.

"Dad seems to think so. I can give you the addresses of some of the larger ones, although I have to say, you don't strike me as someone who's interested in tall buildings—unless, of course, it's to have your superhero boyfriend leap over them in a single bound."

"I don't have a superhero boyfriend," she informed him tersely.

She was rewarded with a killer smile. "Sounds promising," Josh told her.

"Well, it's not," she said, making things very clear right up front. "You said I didn't strike you as someone who would be interested in tall buildings. Just what do I strike you as? And I warn you, I can see a line coming a mile away."

"Good to know," Josh responded, then said, "One won't be coming."

Lacing his fingers together before him, Josh leaned his chin on them as he studied her for a long moment, his brown eyes sweeping over her slowly as if he was literally taking measure of every inch of her.

Finally, he told her the conclusion he'd come to.

"I'd say that you were someone who was interested in art. Passionately interested, would be my guess," he amended.

"And just how did you arrive at this 'guess'?" Leonor questioned.

"That's easy," he assured her. "By the way your pupils dilated just now when I mentioned my art collection. I definitely got your attention. Let me guess—you're a collector yourself."

Eventually, she wanted to be. But that wasn't in the cards just yet. For now, she was content to soak up knowledge and experience. "Not exactly."

Leonor paused just then as the server approached their table with a basket of bread sticks.

"Would you like to order something to drink?" the woman asked.

The idea of having something stronger than the water that was already on the table was highly appealing to Josh, but he knew he couldn't afford to be anything but sharp right now. He looked at Leonor, waiting for her to go first.

"Just a lemonade," she told the server.

"Make that two," Josh said.

"You can't like lemonade," Leonor protested, thinking the man was just trying to be polite.

"I can't?" Josh asked. He looked at her, puzzled. "Why not?"

"Seriously?" she questioned.

"Why? Does liking lemonade make me less of… an art collector?" Josh finally asked, although that wasn't the first thought that came to his mind.

His question made her laugh and he silently congratulated himself on managing to peel away the first protective layer that Leonor Colton had wrapped around herself.

"Being an art collector has nothing to do with it," she told him. "No, it's just that I don't know of any men who would admit to actually liking lemonade, say, over an alcoholic beverage."

His smile was easy, engaging and almost incredibly guileless, Leonor thought as he told her, "Then consider me your first."

Your first.

The way he said the words had her catching her breath just for a second. She had no idea why she was putting a far more sensual interpretation on them, but just for a moment, she had.

And then she forced herself to shake it off.

Collecting herself, Leonor searched for something to say. "What are you doing in Shadow Creek, if you don't mind me asking?"

"I don't mind," he assured her. He broke off a piece of his bread stick before saying, "I'm just taking in the sights."

She gave him a dubious look. He was trying to pull her leg.

"Shadow Creek doesn't have any 'sights.'" She supposed that to some, that wasn't entirely true. But there was nothing here that would make it to the pages of a "must see" section of any reputable guidebook. "At least not the kind that would be of any interest to you."

Josh deliberately looked at her for a long moment. Long enough to make her shift in her seat ever so slightly.

And then he said, "You'd be surprised."

Chapter 3

Josh shifted the focus of the conversation away from him and back to her. "You know, you still haven't told me your name," he reminded her.

She wasn't convinced that this was just an accidental meeting and that he didn't know who she was. Looking up from her menu, her eyes met his.

"No, I haven't."

He proceeded carefully. "Oh, a lady of mystery, is that it?"

Amusement highlighted his rather rugged features. Leonor couldn't make up her mind if the sexy stranger was having fun at her expense, or if he was just talking. Obviously he hadn't heard the hostess call her "Ms. Colton."

"Why don't I call you 'Kate'?" he suggested gamely.

"I've always been partial to 'Kate.' It's my mother's name," Josh explained.

"It's Colton," Leonor said out of the blue. She watched his expression carefully.

It didn't change. There was no enlightenment evident on his face.

"First or last?" Josh asked casually.

This being Texas and an era given to unique names, she supposed it might have been reasonable for him to assume that Colton could be a first name—but she still doubted it.

"Last," she told him. Pausing, she took a breath, mentally bracing herself for the reaction she expected to come, then said, "Leonor Colton."

There was no telltale smirk, no sign of recognition, no change in his expression whatsoever. Had the man been living in a cave? Her mother had made news in every sort of medium with her escape.

"Doesn't that mean anything to you?" she wanted to know.

There was just the slightest regretful rise and fall of his shoulders as Josh apologized for his ignorance. "I'm sorry, should it?"

She didn't believe him. This had to be an act. "You've never heard of Livia Colton?" Leonor almost demanded.

Looking just a touch embarrassed, Josh shrugged again. "There was something on the news the other day, but I have to confess that unless it concerns something of international importance—or the art world—I really don't pay much attention to it."

"The art world," Leonor repeated, still highly skeptical that the man she was sharing a table with was on the level. Granted, there were people who lived and breathed nothing but art, but they were men with forgettable faces, not men who infiltrated women's dreams, the way this one surely had to have been ever since he had first started attending school.

"I'm afraid so," Josh told her. "I told you, I'm a collector and an art buff of sorts." His smile widened in direct proportion to his warming up to his subject. "I find that there are amazing displays of discipline evident in the art world. Discipline that can't be found in society these days." And then he flushed, as if Leonor had caught him in an awkward moment. "I'm sorry. I probably sound like a nerd to you."

"No." She quickly discounted his negative assessment of himself. "But you do sound too good to be true," she admitted in a moment of fleeting weakness.

His smile was almost dazzling as he said, "Why, Ms. Colton, are you flirting with me?"

"No!"

Realizing that she had almost shouted out the word, Leonor lowered her voice as she covertly glanced around to see if anyone was looking in their direction, watching them. She'd been trying really hard to maintain a low profile.

No one seemed to be looking in their direction. It was as if they recognized her, but were giving her space anyway. Maybe there *was* a truce in place between the town and her mother's offspring.

She certainly hoped so.

"No," Leonor repeated in a much lower tone. "I'm not. I'm just saying that I never met anyone who proclaimed themselves to be an art lover—outside of the program at the college I attended," she qualified.

Josh laughed softly, amused at the way she had worded her statement. "It's been a long while since I was in college."

"Where did you attend?" Leonor asked. She reasoned that if she asked him enough questions—and this man was lying to her—she could gather together enough ammunition to trip him up.

His photographic memory pulled up the bio that had been worked up for him.

"College of William & Mary," he told her in the same matter-of-fact tone he might have used if he were telling her that he had attended some trade school in the area.

"That's in Mississippi, isn't it?" she asked conversationally, waiting to see if he would agree with her.

"No, it's in Williamsburg, Virginia," he corrected casually.

Anyone could know that, she thought, pushing on. "What did you study?"

"Not nearly as much as I should have," he admitted with guileless honesty. "But I did manage to graduate with a degree in art." A smile that was fond at the same time that it appeared resigned curved his lips. "My father was furious."

He was trying to reel her in and she knew it. Still, she heard herself asking, "He didn't know what you were studying?"

This time, the shrug was rather philosophical. "My father was hoping that if I didn't follow him into the 'family' business, I'd at least become another Thomas Jefferson. He went to school there," he interjected in case she didn't know that.

She wasn't quite sure she followed the logic here. "Your father wanted you to become a president?"

Josh took a sip of lemonade before answering. "Thomas Jefferson was that century's version of a Renaissance man," he told her. "I think my father was hoping I'd emulate Jefferson and become someone who was good at a variety of things, one of which would be at least related to the building trade."

This time she did follow his line of thinking. "Since Jefferson designed Monticello."

Josh grinned, nodding. "You're catching on."

It took effort not to get caught up in the cheerful way her tablemate presented his facts. "You do spin a story," she told him. Then, in case he thought he was charming her, she added, "I think around here, they call that telling tall tales."

"You don't believe me," he guessed, neither annoyed nor disappointed.

Leonor tempered her words. She had to admit that she did find the man entertaining. "Let's just say I have a healthy skepticism."

"I can understand," Josh replied. "A beautiful woman like you being approached by a total stranger would do well to be on her guard." He leaned in over the table as if to share a secret with her. "There are a lot of unsavory people out there."

"You're not going to try to convince me that you're on the level?" she asked, rather surprised, even though she was doing her best not to show it.

"I've always found that the harder someone pushes a point, the more that point is held to be highly suspect." And he was not about to do anything to turn her off. "I'm just content to share a meal and a conversation with a lovely companion."

He saw that she was about to protest the word *companion*, and quickly said, "Speaking of sharing—" The words hung in the air as he put his hand inside his jacket, slipping it into his breast pocket. Josh extracted five photographs. "I wasn't completely forthcoming with you earlier. I'm not here to take in the sights. I'm actually on a combination vacation/scouting trip—although my father questions how I can take a vacation if I don't have a revenue-producing career to take a vacation from." He flashed a grin. "That did sound rather awkward, didn't it?"

She pushed that observation aside, far more interested in the photographs that were in his hand. Leonor had to admit that as much as she was trying to remain above the exchange, or at least *appear* to be above it, the man she was sharing bread sticks with had managed to arouse her curiosity.

Her eyes riveted to the photographs in his hand, she asked, "What's the scouting part of it involve?"

"I'm looking for the proper place to—let's be honest—" he told her with a smile, "*show off* some of my collection."

At that point, Josh carefully spread out all five

of the photographs on the side of the table, creating rather an interesting column.

She didn't want to look as if he had captured her attention, but he most definitely had.

Giving up all pretense of disinterest, she drew one of the photographs closer to her and looked at it, then at him. It couldn't be a photograph of what she thought it was.

Could it?

"Is that a—?" Leonor deliberately let her voice trail off, waiting for the man sitting across from her to fill in the artist's name.

Which he obliged.

"A Jackson Pollock? Yes. I have to admit that I'm more willing to lend that one out than I would be, say, my Van Gogh. Or the Turner." There was a fond expression on his face as he admitted, "I'm probably rather lowbrow in the opinion of a lot of the so-called 'refined' art critics but there's just something about a seascape that moves me."

Leonor drew all five of the photographs closer to her and studied them, one by one, then raised her eyes to his. "And these are originals?" She didn't bother hiding the note of skepticism in her voice.

"They'd better be, considering the price I paid for them." And then he laughed, lightening the moment. "Yes, they're originals. I had two different art appraisers verify their authenticity."

"Two?" she questioned.

He nodded. Picking up a bread stick, he broke it in half before biting into it. "One could have always been bought by the collector supposedly 'selling' the painting. Two different appraisers from different companies are far less likely to be in collusion."

"So, you're a skeptic," she noted. She felt herself softening despite her resolve. It wasn't in her nature to constantly hold everyone at arm's length.

Josh nodded, although he looked as if he took no joy in admitting the fact. "I'm afraid that these days, you have to be. There are a lot of people out there who want to part you from whatever prize possessions they have their eye on." And then he flashed a smile at her. "But I don't have to tell you that."

"Why?" she wanted to know. He *did* recognize her, she thought. Why else would he have just said something like that to her? He was telling her that he knew she was aware of what he was referring to, namely, the blatant fickleness of her neighbors that she had had to endure when that scandal surrounding her mother had flared up.

But that apparently wasn't what he was telling her, she learned.

"Because it's obvious that you find me highly suspect," Josh told her. "You wouldn't be that way unless something had happened to you along the way to make you so suspicious of everyone."

It was her turn to shrug. "Maybe I'm just naturally suspicious."

"A woman as beautiful as you?" he questioned, shaking his head. "I doubt that."

She had no idea what being attractive had to do with it. "You're pretty free with your compliments."

The look that he gave her could have melted a rock—and she wasn't a rock, she thought, doing her best not to succumb.

"Only when they're merited," Josh countered.

He was being much too smooth. There had to be a way to get to him, to unravel all these pretty words before they completely undermined her defenses.

"So if I had a face that could stop a clock—?" She left it up to him to finish.

"I wouldn't tell you that you were beautiful," he said honestly. "I'd shine a spotlight on all your other assets."

"And flatter those," Leonor guessed knowingly.

He inclined his head, as if considering whether he would or not. "If they deserved it, yes."

She decided to reserve judgment on the man for another time. Right now, the photographs he had shown her had her attention.

"You're really looking for someplace to display these paintings?" she asked, a wary note in her voice. She would hate to be taken in by the likes of this Joshua Pendergrass. She knew that the first thing anyone would think was that she had gotten swept off her feet and dazzled by the man's overwhelming good looks rather than by his breathtaking collection.

Josh nodded. "Yes."

She knew she would hate herself if he actually decided to go this route and she lost out, but she needed to know why he hadn't thought of this himself.

"Why don't you just get in contact with the Museum of Modern Art in New York City? I'm sure that they would be more than happy to put your collection on display."

He finished off the second half of the bread stick before answering. "I'm sure they would."

She looked at him. It seemed rather clear to her. "So? Why don't you?"

"Because the entire museum is teeming with works of art," he explained. "The people who come through those halls are almost anesthetized, accustomed to seeing the greats and near greats at every turn they take, every hall they walk through. I think my collection would be better appreciated displayed in a smaller venue. Someplace that isn't quite as overwhelming." His eyes met hers. "If you get my thinking."

"I do," she told him.

She was trying to play it cool, but she had to admit to herself that she was growing progressively more excited, with each passing moment, about the possibilities this man whose path she had crossed represented to her. To the art museum where she worked. She'd certainly had her share of bad luck, but this had to fall under the heading of the most fortuitous meeting she'd ever had.

Deciding to stop being so morbidly cautious, Leonor broached the subject of where she worked to him to see his reaction.

"You know, I work for an art museum."

She expected him to look delighted, or at least extremely pleased. She hadn't expected him to look disappointed—in her.

"Now you're just having fun at my expense, Ms. Colton."

"No, really, I work at an art museum," Leonor assured him. "And please, call me Leonor. When you say 'Ms. Colton,' I expect to turn around and see my mother standing there."

"All right," he agreed, then tried her name out on his tongue. "Leonor." It seemed to all but float between them. And then he got back to the subject under discussion. "I looked this town up before I came here. I don't recall reading that there was an art museum in the vicinity. So, unless that guidebook is out-of-date—"

"It's not," she admitted. "You didn't read anything about there being an art museum in Shadow Creek is because there isn't one."

Josh shook his head, his rather long dark brown hair moving ever so slightly. "I'm afraid you lost me. I thought you just told me that you worked for an art museum—"

"I do, but I don't work here," Leonor clarified before he could get any further. "I work for an art museum in Austin."

"A museum, not a gallery?" he specified, watching her face intently.

She was beginning to think that a lot of people had tried to put one over on this man at one time or another. He came across as smooth, gregarious and charming, but at the same time he seemed rather subtly alert, as if he was waiting for things to go wrong before they eventually went right.

"It's an art museum," she assured him. "It's not as

large as some of the other ones in, say, the bigger cities like Los Angeles, and certainly nothing like the Museum of Modern Art in New York," she allowed. Leonor looked down at the five photographs again. They were all truly beautiful works of art. "But we have several respectable collections on the premises, and I guarantee that we would do your collection complete justice if you wound up deciding that you wanted to display the paintings at our museum."

He nodded thoughtfully, appearing to carefully consider her words. "I'd have to think about it," he told her.

She'd expected nothing less and would have been suspicious if he had said otherwise. "Of course, I understand."

"Meanwhile, I do have to eat," he said matter-of-factly. "And a bread stick only goes so far." He looked around the premises. "Tell me, does the server ever come back after she brings over the lemonade or are we supposed to just fill up on bread sticks? Because, if that's the case, she's going to have to come back with more bread sticks."

"She's supposed to come back," Leonor told him.

Scanning the area, she spotted the young woman who had brought over their lemonades. She appeared to be talking to the two men who were seated at another table across the way. It didn't look as if order-taking was involved.

Leonor was eager to be accommodating—yes, this man she was sharing a table with could still be a fraud, but if he wasn't, the museum where she worked stood to gain a lot if Josh Pendergrass was kept happy.

As long as all it takes is a full stomach, she silently qualified.

Because if it took anything else, or if this was a case of something else being involved other than an art collector looking for a venue to display his collection, then she wasn't interested in keeping this man content, no matter how exceptionally good-looking he was.

A good-looking man was why she had come home to regroup in the first place. Maybe if David hadn't been as handsome or as charming as he was, she would have seen through his ruse a lot sooner and been spared a lot of heartache.

Well, she was never going to be that blind again, Leonor promised herself.

But she was just as determined not to allow what David had done to jade her or color the way she looked at things. That, she knew, would be as much of a tragedy as her running blindly toward making another really stupid mistake.

Catching the server's eye, the next moment Leonor stood up. Raising her voice only slightly, she informed the young woman, "We're ready to order now."

The server looked only moderately embarrassed to have to be summoned this way. She quickly approached their table.

"Very good, Ms. Colton," the young woman said.

Josh pretended to look at her with a measure of

surprise. "So that really is your name?" he asked, taking the server as the final authority on the matter.

Why would he think that she had lied to him earlier? What was the point of admitting that she was part of a family that had the stain of infamy on it if she didn't have to?

"Yes, Colton really is my name," she answered Josh, and for the first time in a long while, she didn't sigh as she said it.

Chapter 4

"Well, you certainly look happy," Mac said when she walked into the ranch house almost four hours later.

It was good to see her like this, the rancher thought. She'd been through a lot. More than her share. It was time for her to find something to smile about.

He crossed over to her. "I'm guessing that taking my advice turned out well for you."

Leonor nodded. Since the outing had been his idea, she'd chosen to come into Mac's house when she got back from town instead of going straight to the apartment over the stables.

Kicking off her shoes, she sank down on the sofa. It creaked slightly, like an old friend murmuring a familiar greeting as her body settled back against the creased leather.

"You were right, Mac," she freely admitted. "It felt good to get out. And, surprisingly enough," she added with a self-effacing smile, "no one felt compelled to throw rocks at me."

That came as no surprise to him. "You were always the nice one, little girl," Mac told her. "Nobody would throw rocks at you—any more than they'd throw rocks at me."

Leonor laughed at his statement as Mac sat down in the far corner of the sofa. "That's because you're not related to Livia by blood," she pointed out. "Besides, let's face it," she added, tongue in cheek, "you're big and intimidating. People in town would be afraid to throw rocks at you. They'd be afraid of the consequences of something like that."

His rich baritone laugh seemed to completely encircle her. "You might have a point," he agreed. "Just remember," he told her, becoming serious, "I have your back, little girl."

His phrasing amused her, as did the nickname he had for her. Rather than bristle or take offense, thinking it played upon her helplessness, she found it endearing. "And any other part of me that needs protecting?" she wanted to know.

Mac nodded. "Absolutely."

"Good to know."

He looked a little closer at her. "You certainly *are* in a good mood," Mac observed. "Did you run into some old friends?"

She sincerely doubted that anyone in town thought of themselves as belonging to that small, intimate group. To be completely honest, Leonor wasn't so sure that any of the town's locals thought of anyone in her family as a friend.

"That would be pretty hard to do," she told Mac, "given the circumstances. But I did meet this man at that new restaurant across from the bed-and-breakfast..."

Mac was instantly alert. "Oh?"

She smiled. Mac was getting protective. She could tell. She knew the signs. She supposed old habits were hard to break.

Considering everything that had happened in the last few months, it was nice having someone looking out for her, Leonor thought. She could have used Mac when David was hovering around, making her completely stupid and blind until it was too late to undo the damage, she thought ruefully.

"Nothing to get excited about," she warned Mac. "From what I could tell, the man's just passing through. We shared a table at a restaurant."

"The restaurant is that crowded?" Mac asked in amazement. He was always interested in how the other businesses in and around Shadow Creek were doing because, eventually, whatever happened to them had an effect on his own ranch. They were all interdependent in one way or another.

"No," Leonor said, negating that and any other theory that Mac might come up with. "He just didn't want to eat alone and asked if he could join me."

"And you agreed?"

She saw that Mac was watching her carefully. What did he expect to see? "Well, I don't exactly have leprosy."

"No," he readily agreed. "But what happened to being leery?" He would have thought after what she'd been through with this David character, she'd be highly suspicious of any man she hadn't known for years. There was no arguing that Leonor was a very attractive young woman, but she was also a Colton and certain precautions always needed to be in place.

"He's an art collector," Leonor told him, as if that single attribute was capable of negating an entire host of sins.

Mac crossed his arms before his chest, looking exceedingly formidable. "And you know this how?" he asked patiently.

She knew how Mac was liable to take this, but all she had was the truth. "He told me."

"And you believed him? Seriously?" Mac questioned. He frowned. He trusted her judgment, but this didn't sound good. "I thought you were the suspicious one."

She made no comment about that. Instead, she explained what had won her over. "He showed me photographs of some of his paintings. He's looking for somewhere to display them."

"So naturally he thought of Shadow Creek?" The dubious look on Mac's face grew more pronounced.

"No, the Austin Art Museum," she answered a bit too sharply.

This wasn't sounding as good to him as it apparently did to her, Mac thought. "In other words, he's stalking you?"

"No," she insisted. "We just kind of ran into one another."

He highly doubted that, but Leonor was a grown woman, capable of taking care of herself—he supposed. If he suggested otherwise, he knew that was liable to blow up on him.

"Uh-huh. Well, as long as you stay alert, I can't see the harm in that," he said agreeably. His expression softened as he looked at her again. "And I've got to say, it's really great seeing you smile again. For a few days there, I didn't think you were ever going to look anything but devastated again. I don't mind saying that it hurt to see you that way,"

She was surprised to hear him say that. "I thought I was doing a good job hiding my feelings."

Mac laughed, shaking his head. "Hate to tell you this, but you weren't." Since she was in such a good mood, he thought she'd be amenable to doing something else. "Listen, I was just thinking. What if we—?"

But Mac never got the opportunity to finish his sentence because at that moment, the front door flew open, hitting the opposite wall with a bang. Leonor's half brother Thorne Colton came in, scowling and for all the world looking like a storm that was about to roll over the plains.

Without Thorne saying a word to his father, his deep brown eyes immediately homed in on Leonor.

"It was you, wasn't it?" he accused. Not waiting for her to answer one way or another—he wouldn't have believed her if she'd said no—Thorne continued his rant. "Never really thought of you as being this selfish, but then, I guess I couldn't really have expected anything else, could I? Given who your mother is," he concluded nastily.

Mac was up on his feet, his usual easygoing expression gone. "Watch your tongue. And don't forget, Livia's your mother, too."

Thorne blew out an angry breath. "And how many times have I wished *that* wasn't true?" Livia's fourth born snapped. The focus of his anger widened, taking in his father as well as his half sister. "What the hell were you thinking, anyway," he demanded, glaring at at Mac, "letting Livia lead you to her bed?"

"That is none of your business," Mac informed him, his voice only growing deeper as he warned his son off, "and whatever else you might think about that part of my life, you wound up being the result of that brief interlude—and no matter what else might have gone down, I wouldn't have it any other way."

Mac's frown deepened as he looked at his son. "Except, maybe, for when you come rolling through here like a clap of thunder. I want you to keep a civil tongue in your head when you talk to your sister," his father warned.

But Thorne was as stubborn in his own way as his father was. The only difference was their chosen decibel range.

"Why should I when she went running off at the

mouth, spilling family secrets to some jerk with a laptop and an internet byline?" Thorne demanded. His eyes narrowed into dark brown slits as he glared at Leonor. "I'm right, aren't I? It was you who sold us all out and told whoever the hell is behind Everything's Blogger everything about us." He didn't wait for her to confirm his supposition. "How much did they pay you?" he wanted to know.

The last question stabbed her right through the heart. "It wasn't like that," Leonor cried.

Thorne pretended to look aghast. "They didn't pay you?" he asked sarcastically.

"Enough!" Mac declared. "She doesn't owe you an explanation," he told his son.

"For splattering the so-called low points of my life all over the internet, thanks to some lurid blogger?" he cried, outraged. How could his father be taking her side? That angered Thorne almost as much as what he'd just accused Leonor of. "The hell she doesn't."

"Thorne!" Mac shouted. The warning note in the rancher's voice was clear.

Unable to take Mac fighting with his son over something that she ultimately was responsible for, Leonor raised her voice to be heard above the two men.

"Stop!" she pleaded. When both men looked at her, she began by answering Thorne's question, really hoping she wouldn't break down in the middle of it. "I thought I could trust him," Leonor retorted, anger and hurt throbbing in every syllable. She could feel tears forming as she continued. "We were supposed to get married—"

"Married?" Mac questioned, looking at her. He looked stunned by this addition. "You left that part out," he told her.

Leonor inclined her head, as if conceding her error. "Sorry."

"You're going to have to do better than 'sorry,'" Thorne told her angrily.

Doggedly, Leonor pushed on with her explanation. "I needed to talk to someone, to get everything I'd been carrying around all this time, like some kind of flesh-eating poison, off my chest.

"People were as nasty to me as they were to you—" she began, looking at Thorne.

His laugh was cold and dismissive. "I really doubt that."

"Let her finish," Mac ordered, cutting his son off.

Thorne scowled, but conceded. "Go ahead," he told his sister grudgingly.

"I needed someone to talk to," Leonor repeated, "and he was there, ready to listen."

"And taking notes," Thorne interjected nastily.

Leonor sighed. Thorne was right, but that didn't help anything or change it. "I didn't know that at the time," she told him. "I had no idea he'd wind up putting it all in a blog and selling it to the highest bidder. I thought he loved me, but he turned out to be an opportunist."

"If you wanted to talk so badly," Thorne said angrily, not fully ready to accept that as an excuse, "why didn't you come to me?"

She looked at him. Was he kidding? They were all

at odds when their mother was carted off to prison. Thorne particularly.

"Maybe you forgot," Leonor pointed out, "but you weren't exactly the friendliest audience to turn to these last few years. I *couldn't* talk to you."

He wasn't about to let her turn this around and blame him.

"Maybe that was because I could never understand how you could still love that woman after everything she'd done. She never *once* thought about how her actions would reflect on us or affect us. Hell, she never once thought about us, period," he reminded his sister angrily. "Yet you went running off to visit her in prison every chance you got," he said scornfully.

Her temper flared. Leonor gritted her teeth together as she ground out an answer to his accusation. "Because nobody else did."

"There was a reason for that!" Thorne pointed out in exasperation. "The woman is evil." Fury had temporarily robbed him of breath. When he got it back, he asked his sister, "Was she grooming you to follow in her footsteps? Was that it, Lennie? Was that why you sold us out like that? Are you helping her now?"

Stunned, Leonor couldn't find the words to answer her brother, to defend herself. What hurt most of all was that Thorne felt she had to.

Mac came to her rescue. "That's enough, Thorne!" he shouted. "I want you to apologize to your sister."

There was cold fury on Thorne's face. "Why should I?" he demanded.

Thorne was furious and he felt he had every right to be. His father was blind when it came to Leonor and his other half sisters, but women could be even more evil and deadlier than men. His mother was living proof of that, he thought darkly.

"Because she doesn't deserve to be treated so disrespectfully," Mac informed his son. "Because if it wasn't for her, neither one of us would be standing here right now!"

Thorne had no idea what his father was talking about. "What's that supposed to mean?" he demanded.

"It's nothing," Leonor said quickly. She knew what Mac was going to say and she didn't want him to. This was a private matter between the two of them, not something she'd done for any sort of credit or recognition.

But Mac wasn't about to allow Leonor's generosity to go unnoted any longer. Thorne needed to know just the sort of person his sister was.

"It's not 'nothing,'" Mac told her. "And it's about time people knew how you came through." He shifted his eyes toward his son. "When the bank was breathing down my neck a few years ago, threatening me with foreclosure because I'd had a run of bad luck and missed a few payments, Leonor used her own money to help bail me out. She paid off the bank." There was gratitude in his eyes when he looked at her. "If she hadn't done that, it would have gone up for sale."

Completely stunned in the face of this information, Thorne could only stare at his father. "You never said anything."

"Not the kind of thing a man likes to advertise," Mac replied flatly. "It wasn't my finest moment. But it definitely was Leonor's," he added, looking significantly at her.

Thorne blew out a breath, completely caught off guard. It was his turn to look contrite. "I didn't know," he said to his sister.

"You weren't supposed to know," Leonor said simply. "I didn't do it because I wanted people to have something nice to say about me. I did it because your father needed help and this was my small way of paying him back for all the times he was there for all of us. For me," she added with affection as she looked at the tall, strapping, dark-skinned rancher. "In a way, you're the parent the rest of us never had," she told Mac.

Mac smiled at her. "You made it easy." And then he turned his attention toward his son. "You want to apologize to her?"

He made it sound like an option, but Thorne knew that it wasn't. And, given what he'd just found out, his father was right. He did owe Leonor an apology. Not for being angry about the blog—she hadn't denied being responsible for that—but for losing his temper with her like that. No matter how angry he was, she didn't deserve to have him ranting at her like that, especially not after she'd helped his father the way she had.

Apologies weren't exactly his specialty and this

one was no exception. He went with something positive rather than dwelling on the negative. “Thanks for helping Dad out.”

“Like I said, it was the least I could do.” Leonor shrugged as if it had been no big deal—because, to her, it hadn’t been. The far bigger deal would have been to just ignore Mac’s plight and move on as if there was nothing wrong. “And I did have the money.”

“But you didn’t have to use it,” Mac pointed out.

He wasn’t a man who took anything for granted. Life was hard and he knew that better than a lot of people. He had no really high expectations, but when the occasional pleasant surprise came his way, he was grateful to be able to experience it.

Leonor looked at the rancher. To her way of thinking, there had never been a choice. It was a matter of doing the right thing, or not being able to live with her conscience if she had chosen to close her eyes and just walk away.

“Yes, I did,” she told him quietly.

“Okay,” Thorne conceded. “I take back everything I just said to you,” he told Leonor. “You didn’t sell us out. But what are we going to do about this character who sold the info to the blog?”

“You ignore him,” Mac said, addressing his words to both of them, just in case his son was getting Leonor all fired up about the man again. He wanted her to let go of her anger over this—permanently.

Thorne was not keen on his father’s input.

“That doesn’t seem right after what they wrote,” Thorne protested.

Mac shook his head. His son was missing the point here. "You go after him in any way, even if it's just to carry on an online war, and all you've done is succeeded in getting more people to pay attention to this jackass's blog. If you want a story to die, the way you kill it is ignore it until it eventually runs out of fuel and burns itself out."

"What if it doesn't burn itself out?" Thorne challenged.

Mac was unwavering in his response. "It will. All things die eventually. Yesterday's news is just that, yesterday's news. Unless, like a scab, you keep scratching at it and making it bleed. Then somebody pays attention to it."

Leonor shivered. "A bleeding scab. Not exactly the most appealing image," she said.

"Maybe not," Mac agreed. "But that doesn't make it any less accurate." And then he took a deep breath, his barrel chest expanding impressively. He considered this topic to be over. "I just bought two new stallions and they were delivered this morning." He looked from Leonor to his son. "You two up for a trip to the stable to meet the new arrivals?"

She'd always loved horses. It was the best part of her childhood. She couldn't think of anything she would have liked better than to see the stallions that Mac had purchased.

"Count me in," she told Mac.

Thorne paused. The fire had settled down in his veins. "Yeah, me, too," Thorne said.

“Well, what are you waiting for?” Mac wanted to know. He crossed to the front door, beckoning them to follow him. “Let’s go!”

Chapter 5

Leonor wasn't in the habit of deliberately ignoring her cell phone. In Austin, even when she wasn't actually *at* work, it was on 24/7 in case her boss needed to get in contact with her regarding one detail or another concerning the museum's operation.

She'd taken her leave of absence because of David's devastating betrayal, and the same day that she had left Austin, she started turning her phone off at night. From there, it was a short hop to generally ignoring her cell during the day. The moment she drove into Shadow Creek, she'd turned off the ringer and the few times that she had felt her phone pulsing, indicating either a call or a text message, she didn't bother picking up—or even looking at it to see whose call she was ignoring.

Her main focus right now was healing.

For all intents and purposes, because of the abyss she had slipped into when she arrived on Mac's doorstep, the outside world had been dead to her. But slowly, with Mac's encouragement, she'd begun to come around and was once again rejoining the human race.

It didn't hurt to have her relationship with Thorne reestablished. And that lunch yesterday that had come about because Mac had urged her to get out of the house and off the ranch had caused her to tap into her people skills once more.

She was finally beginning to feel alive again, Leonor thought.

Which, she recognized, was a fortunate turn of events because the first call she decided to answer on her cell phone came from Sheffield.

Going out onto the front porch for a little privacy, she swiped her finger along the screen, allowing her cell to go into an active mode.

Rather than offering a customary greeting, in the interests of saving her boss time and effort, Leonor got right down to business and said, "I don't think that I'm really ready just yet to come back to work, Mr. Sheffield."

"I see that going home hasn't managed to countrify you," the museum director commented drolly.

She realized that she'd jumped the gun—and should have allowed the museum director to speak first before she launched into her little speech.

"I'm sorry," she apologized. "I thought that was

why you were calling—to find out if I was coming back."

"Well of course I'd welcome that sooner rather than later, but I did tell you to take your time," the director reminded her. There was some reluctance evident in his voice. "But I'm not calling you about that, Leonor. I'm calling to give you a heads-up."

She wasn't sure just what the director was talking about. Leonor didn't know whether to just brace herself or be worried. Doing her best to sound relatively calm, she asked, "About what?"

"There's a billionaire by the name of Joshua Pendergrass headed your way. I'd like you to…" Sheffield paused for a moment, as if searching for the best way to phrase what he wanted her to do. "Get on his good side," Sheffield finally said, hoping the words were vague enough for her to read whatever she needed to into them.

Leonor smiled to herself. Funny how things turned out, she thought. "I believe that I might already have done that."

"You mean he's in Shallow Creek already?" Sheffield asked, surprised.

"Shadow Creek," Leonor corrected tactfully, not for the first time.

It seemed to her that the director had a mental block when it came to getting the name of the small town right. She would be the first to admit that, outside of being the place where the federal agents had captured her mother, there was nothing that could be considered memorable about the town.

"And yes," she told the museum director, "he is."

"You've made his acquaintance?" Sheffield didn't bother hiding the eager note in his voice.

That sounded so formal. The man might be a billionaire, but there had been nothing "formal" about their first meeting. Or, for that matter, the lunch that followed.

"I...um...ran into him at a restaurant yesterday."

"And?" Sheffield wanted to know, urging her to share details.

On a hunch, Leonor decided not to say anything about eating with the man. Instead, she said, "And we exchanged a few words."

"You realize that he's an art collector." Sheffield sounded as if he could barely contain himself. She'd never heard him sound this way before, but then she was aware that the museum was having a rather tough time of it lately. Donations to the museum had been sparse this quarter, causing some belt tightening to take place.

"Those were some of the words we exchanged," Leonor acknowledged.

"Wonderful!" She almost expected Sheffield to burst into applause. Struggling to contain his excitement, the director told her, "I've got it on good authority that he's interested in finding a museum he feels will do his art collection justice. And, if it turns out that he's happy with what we can do to highlight it, I'm sure that we'll be able to get the man to make a sizable donation to the museum."

"That sounds good," Leonor replied.

She knew that she undoubtedly sounded subdued to the director, but she really wasn't certain what it was that Sheffield was looking to hear from her.

"No, Leonor," Sheffield corrected. "That sounds *great.* If Pendergrass gives the museum a generous donation, we can build another wing, attract more works of art and finally have the museum live up to its true potential."

The last part sounded as if he was talking more to himself than to her.

"You didn't call just to tell me all this, did you?" Leonor asked tactfully.

It wasn't really a question. She was trying to coax the director into getting to the point. She really liked Sheffield and he was easy to work for, but the man was given to talking in circles and she didn't want to remain on the phone with him for the next hour or so, waiting for Sheffield to finally get to whatever it was that had made him call her in the first place.

She heard Sheffield sigh and wondered if she'd offended the man by being too direct. It was a fine line and she knew it.

To her relief, the next words out of his mouth told her that she hadn't.

"I want you to wine and dine the man, Leonor. Get him to loosen up. Get him to *donate* as much as possible. That's it in a nutshell," he told her.

"That's rather a big nutshell," she couldn't help commenting.

"Not for you. Don't forget," he was quick to add, "I've seen you with our donors at the fund-raisers we have here at the museum. You could get anyone to loosen their purse strings, even if those purse strings are supposed to be sewn permanently shut."

She was willing to admit that she was persuasive, but she was hardly as good at the job as he was saying. "I think you're giving me way too much credit."

"And I don't think you're giving yourself enough," Sheffield countered. "We need this, Leonor," he told her, trying to appeal to her sense of loyalty to the museum. "You know that museum attendance has gone down in the last nine months. A new wing, new artwork, all that could bring attendance up again." He paused, as if to regroup. "You said you've already met him—"

She was beginning to get an uncomfortable feeling about what he was asking her to do. "Yes, but I can't just throw myself at the man," she protested, thinking that was exactly what Sheffield wanted.

"You're an attractive young woman, Leonor," Sheffield told her in his most cultured voice. "I'm sure no 'throwing' will be necessary." He became impassioned. "Listen, this is practically kismet. He's all but fallen into our laps—your lap," the director corrected, then made another appeal by telling her again, "The museum could really use this boost."

The museum needed a "boost" and Pendergrass just happened to come along, looking for a venue to display some of his art collection. This sounded almost too good to be true. Something was wrong here, she thought. It felt, for lack of a better word, *off*. She couldn't put her finger on it, but she did know that her suspicions were multiplying at a really prodigious rate.

"Mr. Sheffield, you said that this man's a billionaire," she began.

"Yes, that's because he is."

Other than what Josh had said to her during his lunch, she had never heard of him before. Had Sheffield? "How do you know that?" she wanted to know.

"Mr. Pendergrass called here the other day, asking questions about the museum's history, asking all sorts of questions about the employees I have working there. When I asked *him* why he was asking all these questions about the museum, he told me that he was looking into various art institutions in the state. He was trying to find the proper venue to display part of his rather extensive art collection.

"He *also* said that he might even consider donating one or two paintings to the museum once he made up his mind which one to go with. I tried to get him to meet with me, but he said that he was currently headed out to your neck of the woods on business."

She heard Sheffield laugh, delighted with the scenario he was relating. She winced a little. The director was a tall man, but he had a high-pitched laugh that reminded her of a blue jay.

"The second he said that, I felt like I'd stumbled across a leprechaun," Sheffield told her. "Now I need you to get him to take you to where he's hidden his pot of gold."

She was tempted to tell Sheffield that he was *really* getting carried away, but she knew that wouldn't do any good, or change anything. Besides, the man had been good to her. He'd allowed her to work her way up and had been nothing if not encouraging. And there had been other candidates available whom he could have hired as curator, but he'd chosen her.

She owed him.

And, she supposed that "wining and dining" the man she'd had lunch with yesterday couldn't exactly be termed as a hardship. She had enjoyed his company.

"I'll see what I can do," she told him.

"And I'll start putting together that budget for the new wing," Sheffield told her happily.

Talk about pressure, she thought. "Don't start counting chickens before the eggs are even laid," she warned.

"I've got a lot of faith in you, Leonor," Sheffield told her.

He sounded as if he meant it. The next moment, he'd terminated the call.

"That makes one of us," Leonor murmured to herself as she put away her phone.

"You're leaving?" Mac asked when he saw the suitcase on the front porch an hour later. He was clearly surprised. "I thought that you and Thorne had patched things up."

"Oh, we did," she assured him.

"Then you're going back to Austin because your leave of absence is over?" Mac guessed, trying to determine why she was leaving so abruptly.

She wasn't about to lie to him. Besides, there was the possibility that they'd run into each other—or that one of her siblings would see her and report back to Mac that she was in town, not back in Austin.

"No, not yet," Leonor answered. "I'm just going to be moving into a bed-and-breakfast for a few days."

Mac was obviously confused. "I don't understand. Unless you needed to get back to your job, I thought you understood that you were welcome to stay here at the ranch for as long as you want while you're in Shadow Creek."

"And I appreciate that," she was quick to tell him, "but I don't want to wear out my welcome and I don't want to get underfoot." She felt guilty about taking the easy way out since neither one of those excuses she was giving him were the real reason why she was moving.

Mac was quick to shoot down the excuses. "That's not going to happen and you know it." He could tell that she was hiding something. He could always read her better than he could any of the others. "What's really behind this move of yours?"

If she told him that she was doing it to get closer to Pendergrass in order to facilitate getting a donation from the man, it sounded as if she was allowing herself to be pimped out by the museum director, and that really wasn't the case.

She tried again.

"Let's just say I need to stand up on my own two feet and I need to take baby steps in order to do it.

This way," she added with a warm smile, "you're right here if I need you."

He looked at her for a long moment, not completely convinced by her story, but willing, for now, to allow the excuse she was giving him to stand. "Okay, little girl, I won't argue with that. As long as you remember that you can *always* come back to the ranch. Day or night," he underscored.

"I know that." She brushed her lips against the man's rough cheek. "And I really appreciate knowing that I can. You're one in a million, Mac.

"I'll give you a call once I'm all checked in," she promised.

About to leave, she stopped, doubled back and gave Mac a quick hug. "Thank you for everything."

Mac brushed off Leonor's words. "There's nothing to thank me for, little girl. We're family, remember?" he asked simply.

For some reason, hearing him say that, especially when the rest of the family had practically gone into hiding at one point or another, made her teary.

Leonor left quickly before she started to cry.

She would have preferred staying on Mac's ranch until she was ready to return to Austin and work, but with this "assignment" that Sheffield had given her, she knew that she would have more of a chance of crossing paths with Joshua Pendergrass if they were staying at the same bed-and-breakfast At least this way she had an excuse for being on the premises, sitting in the lobby or at poolside, watching for him.

Coming into town from the ranch every day was difficult without a concrete reason.

She didn't need a reason if she was registered at the bed-and-breakfast.

Admittedly, Leonor still felt somewhat uneasy about having to play up to the man and trying to influence him. However, she reminded herself as she drove into town, at bottom, it was really all part of her job. Her main function was to keep the museum running and for that to happen it needed both funds and displays that would keep the public coming back for more.

A great deal factored into that, not the least of which was generous donations. And, she had to admit that she'd gotten the distinct impression from Pendergrass over the lunch they'd shared, that he was more than willing to open up his wallet if he felt that the museum doing the asking was worthy of a donation.

As she approached town, she murmured under her breath, "Time for you to earn your keep, Colton, and show Mr. Sheffield that he was right in having enough faith in your abilities to hire you."

If she were her mother, Leonor thought, this sort of thing—getting money out of people—would be second nature to her. One way or another, Livia Colton had been separating people from their money all her life without any qualms.

But she wasn't her mother and she was proud that she wasn't, Leonor thought. She just had to stop comparing herself to the woman. What she was doing was legal—and necessary. None of those factors had ever really concerned Livia.

He spotted Leonor Colton the second she walked into the bed-and-breakfast.

Josh had been sitting in the small lobby, covertly watching the comings and goings of both the guests and the people they were meeting. He wasn't exactly sure what it was that he was waiting for—he knew that there was no chance in the world that Livia Colton would come sauntering into the establishment, neither larger-than-life, nor swaddled in a disguise.

But he had this feeling that if he watched long enough—and was patient enough—Leonor Colton might just put in another appearance. After all, she'd already been here once. And he had certainly put out enough bait regarding his so-called art collection to at least capture her attention, if not the woman herself. That, and the call he'd placed to the art director at the museum where she still had a job waiting for her, had planted enough seeds to get her to eventually turn up in his court.

That was what he'd been saying to himself since early this morning when he had positioned himself in this chair in the lobby, facing the B&B's front door, an untouched newspaper on his lap.

And now she was here.

Finally.

Patience, he thought, obviously paid off.

And she was carrying a suitcase, he noted happily. That could only mean one thing. She would be in close proximity.

This made things easier.

Josh congratulated himself on getting one step closer to his target. He would have ordered a drink to celebrate, but things came up and he needed to be thinking clearly at all times.

He was certain that Livia Colton's daughter was here because of his call to her boss. He guessed that she didn't want to be overly obvious, but she was here to get close to him.

He smiled to himself just before he got up from his chair. They both obviously had the same goal: to get close to one another.

But only he was aware of that shared goal. Knowing that both amused and heartened him.

Josh approached her from the front, thinking that a far better method than just startling her by popping up behind her.

"Hello, Leonor," he said, greeting her. "Do you need help with your suitcase?"

Chapter 6

The whole reason Leonor had left Mac's ranch and gotten a room at the bed-and-breakfast was so that she could "accidentally" run into Joshua Pendergrass without appearing to have orchestrated that accident. But she hadn't counted on that happening the second that she came through the front door into the small lobby. She was still working on her excuse for suddenly changing her location like this. Running into the friendly billionaire the moment she'd arrived had her drawing a temporary and complete blank.

It took her a second to find her tongue. When she did, Leonor realized that Joshua was about to take her suitcase from her and carry it to the reservation desk. She found that highly unusual for a man of his privileged background. She was certain that he had to have people fetching and carrying for him.

"I can carry my own suitcase," she told him, still holding on to her luggage.

He gave her that easy smile she felt had to have been the undoing of every woman who had crossed his path.

"I'm sure you can, but this allows me to practice a little chivalry. Besides," he went on to tell her, "carrying your suitcase brings back memories. I worked in a hotel one summer."

Leonor looked at him, clearly puzzled. Was he making all this up? "Your father let you work in a hotel?"

Josh nodded. "He wanted me to learn about business the hard way, from the ground on up. He'd put me to work in one of his buildings. It happened to be a hotel," he told her.

The first thing he had been taught about going undercover was to stick to the truth as much as possible if he had to go into detail. What he'd just said to Leonor was true—to an extent. He *had* worked as a bellhop one summer, but it was hardly his father's building. A family friend had gotten him the position. That was the summer when he discovered that the wealthiest people usually were the stingiest tippers.

"My father wasn't an easy man to please," Josh went on to tell her. "I think that was the summer I stopped trying."

"Well, at least you had a father to try to please,"

she commented. Hers had died not long after she'd been born.

She put her suitcase down and the reservation clerk came up to the desk.

The tall man greeted her with a friendly smile. "We have your room all ready for you, Ms. Colton." Waiting for her to sign in, the clerk handed Leonor the key to her room. "Second floor suite, just like you requested."

"Second floor?" Josh echoed. He found that rather an unusual request. "This place has three floors. I would have thought you would have wanted a room at the top. The view is better."

"Not me," she told him with feeling. "I like being closer to the first floor. If there was a room available on the ground floor, I would have asked to be put in one of those."

"Fear of heights?" he guessed, curious what the motivation behind her choice was.

Taking possession of the keycard, Leonor turned away from the reservation clerk and lowered her voice so that only Josh was privy to her answer. "Actually, it's a fear of fire."

His eyebrows drew together, forming a perplexed furrow. "Come again?"

She saw no harm in explaining her reasons. "I saw this old, classic movie when I was very young and unfortunately, very impressionable. It was about a fire that broke out in this incredibly tall skyscraper. It absolutely terrified me and kept me up for *nights*, remembering that awful crackling noise. I even begged my older brother, Knox, to get a fire extinguisher for me. I think he thought I was crazy, but he still managed to get me one." A rueful, embarrassed smile curved the corners of her mouth. "I slept with it next to my bed for the next six months."

"Well, that's a new one to me," Josh told her with a laugh. "When most beautiful women talk about their first bedmate, it usually isn't a fire extinguisher."

There was a slight, vague shrug of her shoulders as she said. "My family's very unique."

"I wasn't thinking about your family." He glanced down at her suitcase, then picked it up before the clerk could dispatch a bellhop to do it. "Since I've got your suitcase, would you mind if I accompanied you to your room? You can leave me at your door if you'd like," he told her.

Leonor smiled at him in response, wondering why there were suddenly butterflies doing field exercises in her stomach. She was thirty-one years old, she silently argued, and the last time she'd felt butterflies fluttering in her stomach, she'd just turned fifteen and had a crush on one of Knox's friends.

"I'm sure you'll be on your best behavior," she said. "And if you're not, you know I could always take you to court for one of the paintings in your art collection as restitution. I'm sure that's a great incentive to behave."

"You never know." His eyes met hers momentarily. "It just might be worth it," he said as he got into the elevator with her.

Because of the time of day, they had the elevator

to themselves. The butterflies in her stomach seemed to grow a little larger, their wings crashing into one another.

Josh noted the color rising along her throat, spreading to her cheeks. Watching, he found himself fascinated. He had no idea that there were females over the age of five who blushed anymore. At least none of the women he had known ever did. "Sorry," he told her, "I didn't mean to make you uncomfortable."

"You didn't," she protested.

And then she caught sight of her reflection in the stainless-steel elevator door just before the doors parted. Their eyes met in the reflection for a split second before they found themselves on the second floor.

"Oh, that," she murmured self-consciously, stepping out of the elevator car. "I'm very pale," she said needlessly. "Sometimes, when someone says something that might be embarrassing under different circumstances, I—"

"You don't need to explain," he told her. "And for the record, I think it's kind of charming."

"Now you're just making things up," she told him. She turned to make a right down the hall.

"Um—"

She noticed that Josh wasn't following her. Since he was still holding her suitcase, she thought his immobile stance to be a little odd.

"What?" she asked.

Very politely, he pointed in the opposite direction. "Your room's that way."

She would have asked him how he could know

that, but most likely he'd been here at least a couple of days.

"Oh." This time she didn't even pretend not to be embarrassed. Errors of this sort were a way of life with her. "I have no sense of direction," she confessed. "Given half a chance, I'd get lost in my own closet."

"Must be a big closet," he commented, amused.

"Not really."

He did his best not to laugh, not wanting to offend her.

A few minutes later, after locating her room, Leonor inserted her key, then opened the door. Pausing, she looked at Josh over her shoulder. "Would you like to come in?"

Josh kept a straight face as he asked, "Given what you said earlier, how do I know you won't try to get me at a disadvantage? Say you tried to have your way with me just to get one of the paintings in my collection as restitution?"

"Is that what you really think?" she asked, not sure if he was kidding.

"No, just teasing you. I think you're trustworthy. And I'm always on my best behavior."

"Are you?" she questioned, tongue in cheek.

"I guess you'll just have to trust me," Josh told her seriously.

He saw something flash in her eyes just then, a look of almost overwhelming sadness. She suddenly looked so vulnerable, he had the urge to put his arms around her and try to make her feel safe.

First time that ever happened, he couldn't help thinking.

"Did I say something wrong?" he asked her. He wanted to clear up whatever had just gone wrong before this whole venture took a turn for the worse. "Because if I did, I'm sorry."

"No." Leonor shook her head. "It's nothing that you said."

"Are you sure?" Josh pressed. "Because for a second there, you looked, I don't know—shell-shocked, I guess, would be the best way to describe it."

He looked so concerned that Leonor found herself touched. She supposed that there was no harm in making a general admission. It might even make the man feel beholden to her in some small way, she reasoned. In turn, she could leverage that to get Josh to behave favorably toward her museum.

Oh, Lord, Leonor thought, a wave of fear suddenly washing over her. Was the unthinkable happening? Was she starting to act like her mother? Seeing and judging everything in terms of her own advantage?

"Are you sure that you're all right?" Josh asked, peering closely at her face.

She had to tell him something or he was going to think that she was some kind of a nutcase, Leonor thought. And if he thought that, she was certain that he'd start putting distance between them.

She couldn't let Sheffield and the museum down this way.

Taking a breath, she began to explain, framing it in general terms to stay on the safe side.

"When you said 'trust me,' it reminded me of something. Of someone," she amended. "He said the same thing to me—just before he turned around and betrayed that trust in a really major way."

There it was again, Josh thought, that vulnerable look. Either Leonor was quite an actress and had learned to perfect that look by practicing it in a mirror—or he had inadvertently managed to stir up something painful from her past.

Never changing his expression, he made a mental note to look into Leonor's background a little more thoroughly than he already had.

"I'm sorry you had to go through that. Nothing worse than having someone lie to you," he told her, adding just the right amount of compassion to his voice and trying not to think about the fact that he was doing exactly that for what he'd convinced himself were noble reasons. "Let me make it up to you," he offered.

Putting her suitcase—unopened—into the closet, Leonor looked up at him sharply. "Why? You weren't the one who lied to me."

Hold on to that thought, he told her silently.

"No, but I said something to remind you of that." He smiled at her. "The least I can do is take you out to lunch."

For a moment, her better instinct rose to the surface and she was about to tell him that he didn't have to make any sort of restitution. But the thing was, she knew that she needed him to feel obligated to her in some fashion. She needed to build some sort of a relationship with him, and having him take her out to lunch could very well be the start of that.

Most of all, she needed to get him to trust her so that he would be more than amenable to the idea of working with her *and* her museum. She'd taken on this assignment willingly—after all, the museum had become her baby, too—but there was just this slightest tinge of guilt pricking at her conscience.

Guilt because, at bottom, she was attempting to manipulate Josh. She wasn't that kind of person, she thought.

The man is an art collector and he's extremely wealthy. You're not robbing him; you're finding a way to make him feel good about sharing that collection and his wealth. Nothing wrong in making someone feel like they're making a worthwhile contribution to society. Stop trying to put yourself down.

She closed the closet door and crossed over to him. "I wouldn't want you to feel obligated," she began, her cadence just slow enough for Josh to cut in if he wanted to.

He did.

Josh told her, "There are worse things than feeling obligated to a beautiful woman. Speaking of worse things..." he said, suddenly recalling. "Downstairs, just before you checked in, when I told you that there was no pleasing my father, you said that at least I had a father to try to please. What did you mean by that? Wasn't your father around very much?" he asked her, forgetting for a moment that she had told him earlier that her father had died shortly after she was born.

"I wouldn't know," Leonor replied in an offhanded manner, successfully hiding the fact that it bothered her. "My father wasn't around long enough for me to form any sort of an opinion about him one way or another. He died shortly after I was born. Probably was the only way he could escape my mother," she added wryly.

Bingo!

Utilizing the poker face that had always served him well in the field—and at a poker table—Josh asked, "Your mother was a hard woman to get along with?" He made a point of not sounding overly interested in her answer. "Look, if I'm prying—"

"No, it's all right," she told him. "My mother's a puzzle no one has learned how to solve yet. And there was no pleasing her because no one ever knew what she liked. We still really don't," she added in a quiet voice, saying it more to herself than to the man standing in her room.

Leonor blinked, suddenly realizing that she had loosened the reins a little too much. This was just what she hadn't wanted to do.

"I'm sorry. How did I suddenly start talking about my mother?" she asked self-consciously.

Josh knew just what to say. "I think we were comparing unhappy childhoods."

She laughed at that, and then shook her head in disbelief. She'd promised herself not to talk about her family and here she was, doing just that. Granted, it was in general terms without any real details, but the fact was that she *was* talking about her mother, and she knew that the subject had to be off-limits for her if she was going to get on with her life.

"Did I say something funny?" Josh asked. "I really need to know so that I can do it again later," he explained. And then he smiled as he told her, "You have a really nice laugh."

That was a line, Leonor told herself. It *had* to be a line.

And yet, it sounded so natural, so genuine, she could have sworn that he meant it.

Found herself *wanting* him to mean it.

Careful, Lennie. You can't be wanting him to have any sort of feelings for you. This is what they call getting caught up on the "rebound." You don't want to get tangled up in something like that because then you're guaranteed to make really stupid mistakes, mistakes that might even be worse than the ones you made with that monster, David. And you know how that turned out.

Don't you ever learn?

Regrouping, Leonor offered the man in front of her a polite, albeit slightly frosty, smile.

"You know," she told him, "you should save those sorts of compliments for your girlfriend, or better yet, your wife."

"That would be good advice, if I had either one of those," Josh replied. "But I don't."

Okay, that just wasn't possible, Leonor thought. *Look at the man.* "I don't believe you."

Josh Pendergrass was drop-dead gorgeous, as well as young and apparently very wealthy. He also seemed very nice. That was above a trifecta in any woman's book. It also made him fair game. How could he possibly not have at least a girlfriend?

"It's true," he told her. "There's an ex-wife in the picture," he said, recalling what Bailey had put down on the Facebook page he'd created for him. "But we were married much too young, and neither of us understood what it took to make a good marriage."

"And no girlfriend?" Leonor pressed.

Getting into the part, he knew the pitfalls that existed in the world he professed to belong to. "What, you think because I'm rich it would be easy for me to have a girlfriend?"

Since Josh was the one to bring it up, she didn't have to tiptoe around the subject. "Basically, yes, I do."

"Well, actually, it's just the opposite," he told her. "When you have the kind of resources I do, the kind that attract major attention, you never know if someone is attracted to you or to your money. You would be surprised how many people, especially women, will say anything, do anything, just to get close to me—and the zeroes in my family's accounts."

"Poor little rich boy?" Leonor asked. Though she actually tried not to, she couldn't help the sympathetic note that entered her voice.

He inclined his head. "Something like that," Josh agreed.

She was trying to make light of it, but she couldn't. Because there it was again. That sharp twinge of guilt, the same one she'd felt before, pricking at her conscience.

And at the same time, she found that she could totally relate to this man, especially when it came to this subject. Because she'd been in the same situation. She'd had people pretend to be her friend just because she was Livia Colton's daughter, the daughter of a woman who fairly reeked of money and connections. At one point there were all sorts of people trying to become her friend—until her mother's sudden fall from grace. Then, just like that, she and her siblings, as well as Livia, became the town lepers. People just couldn't get away from them fast enough.

It took close to ten years to change that. She had no idea how many more years it would take to heal the wounds that were left behind.

"You know," she told Josh in a quiet voice, "the more I talk with you, the more I realize that we have a great deal in common."

"You're just saying that to make me feel better about my life."

"No," Leonor contradicted him. "I'm saying it because it's true."

Chapter 7

Joshua Howard knew his superior at the FBI considered him to be very good at his job. He knew how to lose himself in whatever identity he took on. But more than that, he knew how to focus attention on the subject of his investigation so that he or she felt as if he was really interested in them and what they had to offer by way of insight into the human experience.

Leonor Colton, however, quickly turned out to be an unexpected challenge. Not because he was losing his touch or was overplaying his hand, but because she seemed to be suspicious if he displayed too much interest in her. Unlike most people or any of the people he had ever set out to investigate, Leonor didn't really like to talk about herself.

So, when they went out for that lunch he had promised her and he asked her what seemed like a very casual question—what had attracted her to art in the first place—Leonor very cleverly turned the question right back at him.

"What attracts anyone to their field of interest?" she asked Josh. "For instance, what made you start collecting works of art?"

"Because I could," he answered, then flashed a self-deprecating smile that, even though she tried to block it out, Leonor had to admit she found exceedingly engaging. "I know that probably sounds pretty pompous and conceited to you—"

"No, not really," Leonor said a bit too quickly, not wanting to seem judgmental in his eyes.

To her surprise, Josh laughed. "Then you would be in a class by yourself because most people would say that I was being exactly that." And then he explained his earlier, flippant answer. "Fortunately, for me, money was never an obstacle." Just in case she thought he was bragging, Josh told her, "My father was busy building his empire. My mother was busy being a socialite whose favor everyone was always trying to cultivate.

"Occasionally, they recalled that they had come together long enough to create a child, and to appease their consciences for neglecting that child, they gave that child—me—free rein for the first twenty-five years of my life. Oh, I was sent to the right schools, was seen with the right people—all that window dressing was my camouflage while I was seeking my own path, going my own way."

He still hadn't really answered her question. She was sure he had to have had a reason and she was interested in hearing it—unless, for some reason, he was lying to her and was only pretending to get close to her for some ulterior motive. She'd been through that—big-time—once, and she didn't want anything like that to happen again.

"But why art?" Leonor pressed. "Why not—" She cast about for something that was the opposite of the way of life he'd chosen. The way of life she mentioned was one that she highly disapproved of. "Why not a life of gambling and strippers?"

"Not that those don't have a great deal of appeal," Josh told her, humor glinting in his eyes. "But art—paintings—captures beauty. Permanently captures it," he emphasized. "I have to admit that I like the idea of owning beauty. Of being able to display it and to have people know that what they're looking at belongs to me—as much as anyone can actually own works of art," he added wryly.

She wasn't sure she quite got his meaning. "Then you *don't* own it?"

"Oh, I do," Josh assured her. "But in a sense, works of art belong to everyone," he said, a smile curving the corners of his mouth.

There was a basket of hot, crusty bread on the table and she was slowly taking apart the slice she had chosen, eating it a tiny piece at time.

"I have to say," she told him after taking another small bite, "your perspective is rather unique."

"That's what my father said, except without the

charming smile," Josh added. "Are you sure I can't interest you in a glass of wine?" he asked, ready to signal the server to come to their table.

"I'm sure," she replied.

"Then you're a teetotaler?" he guessed, raising an eyebrow as he posed the word.

She had nothing against drinking once in a while—with the right person, which in this case would have been someone she knew. She really didn't know him yet.

"Not really, just careful," she told him. "Alcohol tends to impair judgment."

"Are you saying that you don't trust yourself?" he asked, a glint of a smile on his lips.

Was she implying that she was capable of throwing herself at him if she was the slightest bit inebriated?

That would be useful, he thought. He also found the thought very appealing.

Her eyes met his. Hers were *not* smiling. "No, it's not myself that I don't trust."

"Ouch." Josh pretended to wince. "Was I just put in my place?"

"Not you specifically," she told him. She was, after all, trying to cultivate him as a donor for the museum, Leonor reminded herself. She couldn't lose sight of that. "Let's just say people in general."

"But you're not having lunch with 'people in general,'" Josh deftly pointed out. "You're having lunch with me—and I assure you that I am very trustworthy. Besides," he pointed out as the busboy came to clear away their plates and the near-empty breadbasket, "we're not exactly sequestered on a yacht in the middle of the ocean." He subtly gestured around the dining room. "We're in a very public place. I'm not about to try anything—no matter how tempted I might be," he added in a slightly lower voice.

She told herself that the air was too dry in the restaurant and that was the reason she was having trouble catching her breath. It had nothing to do with the exceptionally good-looking man who was quite clearly flirting with her.

Clearing her throat, Leonor said, "I'm not worried about that."

He looked at her for a long moment. "Then what are you worried about?"

She could feel her defenses heightening. "Who says I'm worried about something?"

He was determined to take down that wall that Livia's daughter had surrounding her—one brick at a time if necessary.

"Please, I do have some people skills and there's something definitely on your mind," Josh insisted. His tone was patient as he said, "I've been told that I'm a good listener."

Even though he did get her pulse up several notches, she'd been studying him at the same time. He wasn't uncomplicated by any means.

"That's probably because you don't talk very much about yourself, preferring to have people monopolize the conversation talking about themselves," Leonor astutely observed.

This woman promised to keep him on his toes, Josh thought.

"Touché," Josh said with a laugh. "But, just so you know, I was taught that talking about myself was the height of conceit—that's why I'd rather listen than talk. But if there's something you'd like to ask me, go right ahead," he encouraged. "Ask."

All right, she had a question for him, Leonor thought.

"What are you *really* doing here, Josh?" she wanted to know.

His smile was quick. "That's easy. Soaking up the atmosphere."

How dumb did he think she was? "Shadow Creek doesn't have any 'atmosphere,'" she countered. At least not the kind that would interest someone like Joshua Pendergrass. She waited for his next move.

He surprised her by asking, "You don't really believe that, do you?"

It wasn't actually an accusation, but she could feel herself wiggling inside anyway. "Why wouldn't I?" she wanted to know.

"Because you're beautiful, young, cultured and educated. You could write your own ticket to anywhere. And yet, you're here." He'd almost slipped and said, "And yet, you came back here," but he caught himself just in time. She'd be on to him then, because there was no reason for him to know that she had left Shadow Creek years ago and had only recently returned—right after her mother's escape from prison.

"I have family here," she told him. It was the first

thing that came into her head. The fact that it was also true and what had motivated her to come back was more than she wanted to say at the moment.

But apparently Josh was not finished asking his questions.

"Are you close to your family?" And then, before she could say a word, he surprised her by raising his hand to silence her. "Hold that thought," he requested. "Do you want dessert?" The question had come out of nowhere.

In general, she wasn't a big fan of desserts. It had to be something exceptional. "It all depends on what dessert is," she told him honestly.

He smiled. "My thoughts exactly." Catching their server's eye, he beckoned him over. Once he was at their table, Josh told him, "The lady and I would like to know what you have on your dessert menu."

Obviously prepared for this sort of question, the server recited a number of choices. When he mentioned tiramisu, Josh heard a little sigh escape Leonor's lips, even though her expression never changed.

"We'll have two servings of tiramisu, please," he told the server.

The latter nodded. "Very good, sir." And with that he all but bowed as he retreated, moving backward from the table.

Leonor looked at Josh. "What made you order that for me?"

"Easy," he told her. And then he smiled. "You sighed."

She wasn't aware of making any sound. She'd deliberately concentrated on appearing nonchalant to counteract the fact that she was starting to feel more and more flustered around this art collector she was trying to bring into the fold.

"I did not," she protested.

"Want me to call him back?" Josh offered, pretending to start raising his hand in order to signal to the server. "You can change your order."

"No," she said a bit too quickly. She really did like tiramisu a great deal. "That's all right." And then she looked at him a bit closer and said, "You're very observant."

"That's my art training," he told her with an easy smile. With the dessert issue settled, Josh focused his full attention on the woman he had singled out as the most likely one to have helped orchestrate Livia's escape. "You were about to tell me if you were close to your family."

"No, I wasn't," she contradicted. "You just assumed I was going to tell you."

He twisted the facts just a little. "Then you're not close to them," he guessed "innocently."

He was putting words into her mouth, she thought. "I didn't say that," she protested.

His eyes met hers and he looked at her almost soulfully, throwing her off her guard. "What did you say?"

She didn't want to jeopardize the artwork or the possible donations that hung in the balance, but she had to get answers to the questions that were occurring to her.

"Why would you want to know if I'm close to my family or not?" What possible difference could it make to the man?

The look he gave her was almost pure innocence. "It's called making conversation. It's what someone does when they want to get to know someone."

Was he actually saying what she thought he was saying? She put the question to him. "And you want to get to know me?"

He found that he really didn't have to try too hard to be convincing as he said, "Very much."

Damn David, Leonor thought. Damn him for ever coming into her life. If it wasn't for him, this would seem like the beginning of something really nice. Instead, Leonor found herself being on her guard, afraid of being too trusting. Afraid that whatever she might say to Josh would wind up reappearing online somewhere in a damning article.

Or worse.

"Why?" she heard herself challenging him.

Someone had really done a number on her, Josh thought. Was it because of her mother? Or was all this just a very well-crafted act on her part? He knew which side he wanted to believe, but for the sake of the assignment, he had to proceed cautiously.

"Well, the standard reason would be because you're a beautiful woman and anyone would want to get to know more about you," he told her. "But I've also got another reason."

Okay, here it comes, Leonor thought, bracing herself. *This is just another con job.* "And that reason would be—?"

"You're a curator at the Austin Museum of Art," he said matter-of-factly. "I'm considering having some of my collection displayed there, not to mention that if I'm satisfied with the way they—and I—are treated, I might be interested in making a contribution to the museum itself. Museums can always use contributions," he told her knowingly. "It's a given. There's always something that needs doing, restoring, or building up." He smiled at her. "Am I right?"

There was no point in her denying it because it was true. "Yes."

Well, that was easy enough, he thought. "Good. Then why don't we stop shadowboxing with one another, let down our hair and be honest with each other?" he suggested. "I might not be the kind of son my father wished for but he did teach me one thing." Josh looked into her eyes as he deliberately made his point. "I don't jump into business associations blindly without knowing exactly who I am dealing with."

Leonor inclined her head. She couldn't very well argue with that. "Makes sense."

His smile was victorious. And incredibly seductive. "Thank you. I think so. So," he said, getting back to his initial question. "Are you close to your family?"

She used to be, but there was no point in saying that. Just as there was no point in talking about what had suddenly split their family unit at the seams.

So instead, she merely said, "I'm working on it." And it was true. She really wanted to be there for the others. Their mother certainly hadn't been, and as the oldest daughter, she felt that it was up to her to make up for that.

Josh pretended to think over her words, and then asked, "So, there are hard feelings?"

To put it mildly. There were members of the family that were angry with her, who believed that she had betrayed them. Those were the ones she was going to have to approach one by one and try to win over.

She thought of the awful blog that had caused the huge schism between them. "Misunderstandings," she corrected.

The word could mean anything, he thought. She wasn't one to admit to anything readily. His instincts told him that she was going to have to be won over slowly—one good deed at a time.

"Anything I can help with?" he asked.

She thought the offer strange since they didn't really know one another. Yet at the same time, it was somehow oddly sweet. Had David not ruined everything the way he had, she might have found herself really drawn to Josh.

Instead, she said the obvious in response to his offer. "I don't even know you."

He shrugged that away. "This could be a way that we could get to know one another."

He had a point and with all her heart, she wished she could just go with it. But fear tethered her. So instead, she decided to toss him a crumb of information and see where he went from there.

"It's nothing," she said with an evasive shrug.

"There was a series of installments by a blogger that was less than flattering about the family. Because a lot of personal things were mentioned, some members of the family thought that the information might have come from me."

He was neither condemning of her, nor absolving of her family. Josh merely asked her one question, "And did it?"

Leonor paused for a long moment, debating whether or not to answer him and if so, *how* to answer him.

Finally she said, "Let's just say that I let my guard down and trusted the wrong person."

He nodded his head as if conferring with himself. "Ah, that would explain it."

She didn't understand what he was getting at. "Explain what?"

"That explains why you keep looking at me as if you're trying to make up your mind whether or not I'm just making conversation—or if I'm mentally taking notes."

Her eyes widened. She wondered if he knew just how squarely he'd hit the nail on the head.

"And?" she asked, curious to see what he was willing to say and just how far he was going to take this analogy.

"I already told you, I'm just making conversation and trying to get to know you. Trying to find out, for instance," he added, "what makes you smile."

She saw his expression change, as if something

suddenly occurred to him. Had the server returned with their desserts?

She looked over her shoulder, but there was no one there. Turning back to look at Josh, she asked, "What?"

"I just thought of a way to make you smile. What if I told you that I've decided to go with your museum? That I want to have part of my art collection displayed there, say, for the next three months?"

They really hadn't discussed that in any sort of length yet. "I'd say that you were prone to making snap judgments."

"Not really," he contradicted. "I do know what I want, though."

Why did her heart skip a beat just then? They were talking about art, nothing else. Certainly nothing personal enough to warrant her pulse going up several notches.

"And what is it that you want?" she asked, watching him carefully, almost afraid of his answer.

"I want to have a reason to get to know you better. A reason that you find acceptable," he added.

Something told her to be careful. A warning system she wished she'd had in place when David was in her life was going off now.

But then, she thought, maybe she was being overly cautious because of David. It was hard to tell.

"So, is it a deal?" he wanted to know, telling her what the next step was. "I call my people and have the paintings sent to your museum for display?"

This was too easy. She'd expected to work a lot harder for this. There had to be a catch.

"And what is it that you want in exchange?" Leonor asked.

He grinned. "Right to the point. A woman after my own heart."

"No, I'm not after your heart," she deliberately corrected. This was not going to get personal. This was business. "What I am after is an answer. What do you want in exchange for allowing the museum to display your paintings?"

"Just the pleasure of your company," he told her.

She didn't believe in fairy tales any more. "And that's it?"

He looked at her in all innocence. "That's it."

It didn't feel right. There was something else going on, something she couldn't put her finger on. "How naive are the women you deal with?"

"Not naive at all. As a matter of fact, they're very calculating." Which was true. The women he'd had to deal with were just that. He figured that, despite her rather dewy look, Leonor numbered among those calculating women. "That's why I find you so refreshing," he continued. "You obviously need my paintings, but you're not being conniving in order to secure them. Tell you what," he said as the server approached with their desserts. "Let's have our desserts, and then go our separate ways. You sleep on what I've just said. If you can find something objectionable about it, I'll tender my apology and you don't have to see me again. Deal?" he asked, extending his hand to her.

She couldn't ask for anything fairer than that, she thought. "Deal."

She slipped her hand into his. The moment she did, a warmth descended over her, bringing with it small, electric shock waves that shot all through her.

She told herself it was just the excitement of securing his paintings for the museum, nothing more. But she knew she was lying to herself because, if she were being honest, there was indeed more.

A lot more.

Chapter 8

When Leonor got back to her suite after what had turned out to be an extra-long, albeit very enjoyable, lunch with Josh, the first thing she did was place a call to her boss. She knew that Adam Sheffield would undoubtedly be anxiously waiting to hear from her.

To be honest, she was rather surprised that the museum director hadn't already called her cell phone while she was still at lunch, asking for an update on the situation.

She was hoping to make this a quick call because lunch with Josh had created another totally unrelated by-product. All that conversation about whether or not she was close to her family had caused her to silently resolve she was going to do everything in her power to make that a reality again—and sooner rather than later.

She had already, although quite inadvertently, patched things up with Thorne. Not because of any direct action between them on her part, but because her brother had learned that she'd bailed Mac out when he had been faced with foreclosure.

Heaven knew she hadn't done that with any sort of an ulterior motive—just as she hadn't shared her family's secrets with David Marshall for any sort of gain, financial or otherwise.

She supposed if she thought about it, one deed did wind up balancing out the other, at least in Thorne's case. Now what she needed to do was approach each of her siblings, one at a time, and try to find a way to make them understand that she was just as much a victim of this awful betrayal as they were. With every fiber of her being, she needed to get them to forgive her, and she didn't care how long it took.

She knew that she would have no peace until that matter was finally settled.

But first, she had to tell Sheffield about her progress with Pendergrass. Blocking out any other extraneous thoughts, she dialed the man's private number on her phone.

There was a slight pause after the call had gone through.

A moment later, she was counting off the number of times Sheffield's phone rang. After the fourth time, she heard a tinny voice mechanically begin to give her instructions as to what to do in order to leave Sheffield a message.

In the midst of it, the instructions abruptly stopped and she heard Sheffield's gravelly voice bark out what sounded like "Hello?" Static accompanied his less than friendly voice.

The connection was noticeably poor, but she didn't have time to call all over again so she just started talking.

"Mr. Sheffield, this is Leonor Colton."

"Leonor!" Sheffield's voice instantly brightened as a hopeful note entered it. "So, what's the story?" he asked her eagerly. "Is Pendergrass loaning us some of his paintings?"

The director didn't sound a thing like his usual restrained self. Things at the museum had to be worse than she thought, Leonor decided. She was happy to give him the upbeat progress report.

"Joshua Pendergrass and I spoke at length over lunch today and I'm happy to say that it seems like he's amendable to displaying some of his art collection at our museum."

"I *knew* I could count on you, Leonor." Sheffield's voice swelled with enthusiasm.

Because of her background, Leonor didn't like counting on things until after they were signed, sealed and, most importantly, delivered. Until then, things could always go wrong.

Counting on something could very well wind up jinxing it. Leonor thought of the wedding she'd begun planning in her mind when she'd been so certain that David was going to ask her to marry him. That hadn't exactly turned out the way she'd wanted it, she thought ruefully.

"It's not a done deal yet, sir," Leonor cautioned the director. But because this was Sheffield and he liked keeping things positive, she added, "But it certainly looks that way."

"It will be. Like I told you, I have great faith in you." She heard the man taking a breath, as if preparing to address another topic. She unconsciously braced herself. Leonor didn't have long to wait. "Was any mention made of, you know, possible donations?"

She could almost *hear* Sheffield crossing his fingers as he asked.

"Pendergrass did mention that if he was satisfied with the way his collection was being handled during the showings, then he'd be amenable to making donations to the museum."

"What did he mean by 'the way his collection was handled?'" Sheffield wanted to know, not quite clear on what was being implied.

"Nothing serious," she assured Sheffield. "He indicated that those would be just some minor details that would be ironed out once he makes the final selection as to which of his paintings he wants displayed at the museum."

Leonor patiently waited for more questions to come her way.

Instead, she heard Sheffield enthusiastically declare, "You hit a grand slam, Leonor."

"Is that a good thing?" she finally asked when

her boss didn't say anything further to follow up his statement.

She heard him chuckling to himself. "Don't watch much baseball, do you, Leonor?"

Sports of any kind, other than horse racing, had never captured her attention. She only watched horse racing because of the sheer grace and beauty exhibited by the animals when they ran. Their strides looked positively fluid to her.

"No, sir," Leonor was forced to admit, "I really don't."

"Well, Leonor, for your edification, a grand slam in baseball is the best thing that a batter can hope for." Praising her like this indicated that her boss was still counting chickens before the eggs were hatched, she thought uneasily.

"He still might change his mind," she reminded Sheffield.

She heard the man blow out an impatient breath on the other end before issuing her an order. "Make sure he doesn't. And let me know the second you've finalized the arrangement." Appearing to lose a little of his trust in her, Sheffield began to say, "If you'd rather that I put in a call to Pendergrass myself—"

"No, that's all right, sir. I can handle this," she said, quickly cutting him off. She knew that Sheffield could be extremely pushy at times and she had a feeling that if the director talked to Joshua, he just might just get him to decide against the deal after all. "I seem to have struck up a rapport with the man. If too many people come at him at the same time, Pendergrass might just shut down," she warned.

She was speaking from experience. Leonor vividly recalled the hordes of reporters—print media as well as blogs or vlogs—who had come after her and her family, trying to corner them in order to secure a few personal words regarding Livia's trial, as well as the charges that she was said to be facing.

The image that stuck with her was that it was like having a swarm of locusts suddenly swirling all around them.

"All right, I'll step back," Sheffield willingly agreed. "But don't hesitate to send up a flare if you find that you need help."

"Don't worry," she told him. "I will."

Saying a couple more words before saying goodbye, Leonor finally terminated the connection. She was relieved to have that over with.

Next up, damage control, she told herself. Pendergrass had offered to take her dancing at an intimate little restaurant in the next town. That sounded exceedingly tempting, but she wanted to get started getting back into her family's good graces. The longer she put off talking to the individual members of her family, the harder it was going to be to resolve the so-called problem.

First up, she decided, was her younger sister Jade. The one who, like Thorne and herself, was living in Shadow Creek. She knew she should call Jade first, but that would be giving her sister a heads-up, especially if she indicated that she really didn't want to see her.

This way, she had the element of surprise on her side, Leonor thought. Especially since she intended to come bearing "gifts."

When the family had been torn apart because of their mother's criminal misdeeds and they had all wound up being forced to fend for themselves, four of them had been eighteen or older. Only Claudia and Jade were underage.

Knox, being the oldest, had volunteered to become their guardian, but that meant a lot of sacrifices on his part. He would have had to remain in Shadow Creek rather than uproot his two youngest sisters. It would also have meant that he had to give up his dream of becoming a Texas Ranger.

That was when Mac had stepped up, telling Knox that he would look after the girls. They could remain on his ranch with him until they reached eighteen and could decide for themselves what they wanted to do with their lives.

In Jade's case, the decision turned out to be easy enough. If nothing else, she was her father's daughter. Fabrizio Artero, Livia's last husband, had been an Argentine horse breeder who had Jade on the back of a horse before she could walk.

She adored her father and she took his death a great deal harder than she took her mother's arrest and imprisonment. Being around horses made her feel as if she was somehow closer to her father, so eventually, she decided to open up a ranch for retired racehorses. Hill Country Farms was a place where kids could come to learn how to ride and racehorses were loved and rehabilitated.

Ever the nurturing big sister, Leonor did her homework and found out how many more horses Jade needed at the farm. Then she placed a few calls to make arrangements to get what she wanted. Delivery was swift.

Rather than the usual clothes she had gotten accustomed to wearing as a curator and also when she'd gone out with Josh, Leonor changed into something far more comfortable. Never one to fuss, she put on jeans and a light blue denim shirt, as well as boots, then drove out to her little sister's ranch—whistling.

There were seven years between Leonor and Jade. Added to the age difference, they hardly looked as if they were sisters. Jade had straight, dark brown hair and brown eyes. She stood at five feet six inches and she had what their other sister, Claudia, referred to as a petite frame.

Just as slender as her sister, Leonor was two inches taller than Jade. Only the determined set of their chins gave them something in common physically.

Driving onto Jade's ranch and pulling up in front of the house, Leonor parked her car and marched up the steps to the front door of the tidy little home. She did her best not to appear nervous.

There was a fifty-fifty chance that Jade was home rather than somewhere out on the range or in the stables, so she decided to try there first before she started to drive around.

She lucked out.

Sort of.

Jade swung open the front door in response to her knock, but whatever greeting she was about to offer instantly faded before she could say a word of it.

Not bothering to hide her surprise, Jade looked at her sister and in a less than a friendly voice, asked, "What are you doing here?"

It wasn't exactly the welcome she'd hoped for, but she could make do, Leonor told herself. "I'm here to explain."

Jade started to close the front door. "Nothing to explain," she said coolly. "We all have our own way of surviving."

But Leonor was quick to brace her hand against the door, keeping her youngest sister from shutting it. She expected Jade to be upset, but not this angry. "Jade, please, I didn't do what you think I did."

"You mean sell out the family for thirty pieces of silver?" Jade shot back. "Then how much was it for? What is the going rate for betrayal these days anyway?"

Still trying to keep the door in place, Jade's eyes darted back and forth, uneasily scanning the area directly behind her sister, looking for reporters lurking about. Some of her anger seemed to abate.

"Look, I'm no one to judge," she relented, then said, "Just please leave."

"No," Leonor retorted, digging in. "I'm here now and I want to talk to you."

Jade sighed, appearing to give in. Suddenly, she pulled her sister inside and firmly shut the door behind her, then secured the lock. Leonor thought her sister's behavior was a little strange, but for the time being, she said nothing.

"All right, talk," Jade ordered. Turning on her heel, she led the way into the living room.

Leonor started doing just that. "Whatever you might believe to the contrary, I didn't sell us out, Jade. I was tricked."

Reaching the small living room, Jade swung around to face her.

"How?" she demanded. "Did that guy who wrote those articles tell you that you were playing a word association game?" she asked sarcastically, something that was totally out of character for her.

Leonor felt angry and hurt, but this wasn't the time to display either emotion. Instead, she forced herself to remain calm and rational. She knew this wasn't going to be easy.

"First, he won me over, made me think he cared about me, cared about my feelings." She looked at Jade, trying to make her little sister understand how she felt. "I was really alone after the family broke up. I missed having someone to talk to, to confide in."

I missed you and Claudia, she silently added. But she couldn't reach out to them because, at the time, they were dealing with their own set of problems and she knew that.

"So you picked a *blogger*?" Jade asked her in disbelief.

Leonor shook her head. "I didn't know what he was at the time. I was vulnerable," she admitted none too happily. "And, he tricked me into thinking he loved me, and that we were going to get married—and then he just took off without a trace—but not before he managed to steal my money."

The words sank in. Jade stared at her, stunned. "You're poor?"

"Poorer," Leonor corrected, adding, "In a lot of ways. But not poor," she assured Jade. "He couldn't get his hands on all of it."

Leonor abruptly stopped talking and took a closer look at Jade. It wasn't her imagination. There was something off here. Her sister looked nervous, as if she was waiting for a bomb to go off. Why?

"Jade, is something wrong?" she asked her sister, her voice softening.

"Other than seeing my life and my family's life smeared all over the internet like some poorly written soap opera?" Jade questioned.

"Yes," Leonor said patiently, "other than that."

Jade's chin rose a little bit as she answered with a stoic, "No."

She didn't believe Jade, but she was hardly in a position to accuse her of lying. There was definitely something off here.

Leonor needed to get her little sister to trust her. That, she was willing to admit, very possibly was going to be a slow process.

But there was one thing she could ask Jade right off the bat. Something that was in the back of all their minds, she imagined. "Are you afraid because Mother escaped?"

That was it, Leonor thought. A look had flashed through Jade's eyes, a wary look just like her sister was waiting for that bomb to go off. Their mother was the closest thing to a bomb that either one of them had ever known.

"Aren't you?" Jade asked.

"Yes," Leonor answered truthfully. The admission seemed to clear a little of the tension between them. Leonor decided to move forward. "How's the ranch going?" she asked.

Jade shrugged. "Pretty well."

That was less than enthusiastic, Leonor thought. She knew how much her sister loved being around horses and working with them. There was definitely something off here. She sincerely hoped that her idea would help bring Jade back around to the happy, carefree girl she'd been before the scandal had struck and everything systematically began falling apart.

"Would it be better if you had more horses on the ranch?" Leonor wanted to know.

Seeing that her sister was serious, Jade considered her questions. "Well, we're a pretty small operation at the moment, but I've got plans to expand the ranch," Jade admitted. "As soon as I can raise the funds, the first thing that I intend to do is acquire more retired racehorses."

None of the Coltons had ever had to live on a budget before. But the federal government had swooped in and confiscated all of their mother's land holdings. That had left them all scrambling and trying to make do.

Luckily for Leonor, she thought, her father had left her a trust fund that was entirely separate from Livia's assets.

"Why don't we skip that step?" Leonor suggested. "The one in which you have to wait until you can raise the funds?"

Jade looked at her, thoroughly confused. "I don't understand."

Leonor tried to contain herself, and explain it to her sister slowly. "I was able to secure several more of those retired racehorses," she told Jade. "I thought maybe you could give them a good home here."

"You brought me horses?" Jade asked, still somewhat dazed.

"Well, I couldn't figure out how to gift wrap them," Leonor told her, "but yes, that's the general gist of it. I brought you horses. Oh, you should see them," she said, her enthusiasm growing with each word. "They're all beautiful animals, and now that they can't go on to win races anymore, their owners have just written them off. Their fates were kind of bleak—you know what they do with horses that can't 'earn their keep'—so I thought of you and knew that you could help them."

"How many?" Jade asked uncertainly.

"Five more. To start," Leonor added in case Jade needed more.

"Five," Jade repeated. She shook her head. "I can't pay you."

Leonor felt as if she was making headway. She certainly wasn't going to allow money to get in the way. "I don't remember asking for money."

Jade's eyes met hers. They were full of pride. "I don't take charity."

"Not offering charity," Leonor told her. "The way I see it, you're doing me—and these horses I seem to have acquired—a favor. If you want to give me some sort of payback for them—" Leonor summoned her courage, and then said, "I could use a hug."

Jade laughed softly. "That I can do."

Leonor put her arms out. "I'm waiting."

The two embraced. Leonor blinked back tears. "I didn't sell us out," she murmured against Jade's shoulder.

"I know," Jade finally said, holding on to Leonor for an extra moment.

Jade couldn't help wondering what Leonor would say if she only knew what *she* had done. For a second, Jade was tempted to share, to tell her sister about why she was so very nervous these days. But the moment passed. Secrets were only safe when only one person knew them.

Releasing Jade, Leonor stepped back. "There was still something in Jade's eyes that worried her. Hopefully seeing the horses would change that. "You up to seeing them?"

Jade's eyes widened, not knowing whether or not to believe her sister.

"They're here?" she cried. There was just the slightest note of doubt in her voice.

"They're being delivered here at your stable even as we speak." Leonor grinned. "You know me. I get an idea, I act on it."

"Yes, I guess that I do know you," Jade said with affection, an easy smile fleetingly curving her mouth.

Her sister's smile, temporary though it might be, made everything worth it.

Leonor couldn't resist hugging Jade one more time before they went to greet the farm's newest residents.

Chapter 9

She spent the better part of the afternoon with Jade, and it felt like old times. A time when, despite the fact that their mother was still playing musical husbands and conducting her secret dealings with shady individuals, which allowed her and her siblings to live upscale lives, the Coltons still found a way to make the most of their lives together.

Leonor was happy to see that for a little while, as Jade looked over all five new additions to her stable and acquainted herself with them, she was her old self again. Not the way she was just before Livia was arrested and charged with a whole host of crimes, because at that point Jade had already become almost reclusive and uncommunicative. But the happy, lighthearted way she'd been before her father had died, having been kicked in the head by one of his horses.

"This is really way too much. You're being much too generous, Leonor," Jade protested once the excitement of the new animals' arrival had settled down and the horses had been placed in their new stalls.

"There's nothing generous about it," Leonor told her matter-of-factly. Seeing that her sister wasn't about to accept that, she went on to explain her logic. "You needed more horses and they needed a home. If you have to put a label on it, you can call it matchmaking," she told Jade with a whimsical grin.

"How did you know I needed horses?" Jade wanted to know. Except for a few words, they hadn't really spoken to one another for years now. And all communication had been shut down in the last few months.

Leonor only smiled at her sister. "I have my sources," she told Jade.

The nebulous answer wasn't good enough for her and Jade was about to demand a better explanation than that when it suddenly came to her. And then she understood.

"Mac."

But Leonor pretended to press her lips together, as if sealing in any words she might be tempted to allow to escape. Mac was indeed her main source, but not the only one. She'd been thorough in securing her information.

Leonor shook her head stoically.

"Sorry, Jade, but I've learned my lesson. I know what happens when I accidentally share too much."

Jade looked offended. "Hey, I'm not going to talk to some sleazy blogger."

Leonor's eyes crinkled at the corners as she "surrendered."

"No, you're not. You're my little sister and I want to do this for you. Let me," Leonor requested with sincerity.

Jade sighed. "Well, I guess if it makes you happy..." Jade said, her voice trailing off.

"It does. Very," Leonor responded firmly. She looked toward the horizon. Judging by the sun's position in the sky, it was getting late. "I'd better be getting back to the bed-and-breakfast."

"Bed-and-breakfast?" Jade questioned, puzzled. "I thought you were staying at Mac's. You know, in that little apartment he has over the stables."

"I was. But I'm not at the moment. Long story," she said dismissively. She saw the suspicious look entering Jade's eyes. Not wanting to make any more waves, she quickly added, "It has to do with my job at the museum. I'll tell you about it someday."

With that, she gave her sister another warm embrace, and then hurried out of the stable.

Arriving back at the B&B, Leonor had no sooner entered the lobby than she saw Josh sitting in one of the overstuffed chairs near the registration desk. He appeared to be reading a newspaper—emphasis on the word *appeared*, Leonor thought, because she could see that Josh raised his eyes from the paper the second she crossed the floor, heading in his direction.

Had he been waiting for her?

"Are you stalking me?" she asked Josh in an amused voice.

He folded the newspaper, abandoning all pretense of reading it, but for the moment, he remained seated.

"Well, in the strictest sense of the word, you were the one who came over to me, so if anyone is stalking anyone here, it would look as if you were the stalker and I was the stalkee."

She laughed, shaking her head. The man was in a class all his own. "Is that even a word?"

"Haven't the foggiest," he admitted, this time standing up. He left the paper on the chair in case someone else wanted to look through it. "And, in the spirit of full disclosure, I *was* waiting for you," he told her.

"Oh?" The man had to have enormous patience, she thought, because she could have remained out all day and night, returning in the wee hours of the next morning. "Why?" she asked when he didn't volunteer a reason quickly enough.

"I still hate eating alone and it is getting close to dinnertime."

She glanced at her watch. It wasn't even six o'clock yet. "Just how early do you eat?" she wanted to know, curious.

His smile was extremely sexy, causing her stomach to tighten in response.

"Anytime my charming companion is hungry," he told her. And then he paused as if something had just occurred to him. "Unless, of course, I'm interfering with some previous plans you've made," Josh qualified, giving her a way out.

Since he left the invitation open-ended, Leonor didn't feel hemmed in the way she might have a moment ago. David had been exceedingly attentive to the point that there were times he was practically volunteering to do her breathing for her. Looking back, she realized it had all been part of his plan to win her over and keep her too mesmerized to realize what he was really after: her story and her money.

She shook her head in response to Josh's question. "No, I'm fresh out of plans."

"Then does that mean that you'll have dinner with me?" he asked hopefully.

Even if she felt like digging in—which she didn't—the look on his face would have had her weakening instantly.

"Well, since you've twisted my arm, how can I say no?" Leonor asked. She turned in the direction of the elevator. "Just give me half an hour to freshen up and change."

"Take as long as you like," he encouraged. "Although," he added, "for my money, you look just fine the way you are."

As if to check out his assessment, Leonor deliberately glanced down at herself. She looked exactly the way she had when she'd left Jade's ranch. Worn and dusty. She frowned. How could he want to be seen in public with her looking as if she was a weather-beaten ranch hand? The man obviously had an image to maintain, being who he was.

"I look as if I came fresh off the farm," she complained.

To her surprise, he looked unfazed. "Nothing wrong with that."

Her eyes swept over him. He looked perfect—especially in contrast to her. "In case it escaped your notice, you look as if you came off the cover of an exclusive men's clothing catalog."

His smile was easy. Warming. She struggled not to let it seep into her.

"Don't hold that against me," he told her. "I think I've got a pair of jeans and a denim shirt packed in my suitcase somewhere."

She put her hand on his chest, as if to keep him from going toward the elevators. "Let them stay there. I'll be down in a few minutes."

"I'll be right here," he promised.

Leonor hurried off toward the elevator, telling herself that she was only having dinner with the man to make sure he didn't change his mind about doing business with her museum. This was just a business dinner, she insisted.

The fact that she was smiling from ear to ear and had quickened her step only had to do with her desire to do a good job, Leonor told herself. It had nothing to do with the fact that the second she had seen Josh sitting there in the lobby, her pulse rate had accelerated. That was undoubtedly the result of her hurrying around earlier today, making sure that Jade's horses would be delivered to Hill Country Farms at the same time that she arrived there.

Coordination and her desire to have things as perfect as possible had taken a small toll on her.

Standing next to the chair he'd been sitting in, keeping vigil, Josh now watched as Leonor entered the elevator car.

For just a moment, he had this uneasy feeling that he should accompany her—just in case. It wasn't that he thought she was going to find a way to give him the slip and leave. There was no reason for her to do that. He was good at his job. That meant that he hadn't acted suspicious in any manner, definitely nothing to set her radar off.

But there was something else that was bothering him, and right now he couldn't quite put his finger on it.

Josh glanced at his watch and silently marked the exact time she entered the elevator car. He'd give Leonor half an hour to get ready. If she wasn't down by then, he'd go up to her room and find out what the holdup was. He could always tell her that he hadn't eaten lunch and that his hunger was getting the better of him. Having been at this job for a while now, he knew exactly what to say and how to say it. What was new, however, was this annoying prick of his conscience that kept surfacing more frequently lately.

This was nothing more than a business dinner, Leonor told herself for the third or fourth time as she let herself into her room and locked the door. There was absolutely no reason for her to regard it as anything else.

Certainly not as a date, she silently insisted.

And yet, she couldn't seem to convince the butterflies—they were back—of that. They felt as if they were bigger than ever and they were entrenching themselves firmly in her stomach.

At this point, if they grew even a tiny bit, there wasn't going to be any room left for dinner. That meant that she was going to be able to do nothing more than move the food around on her plate until they were ready to leave the restaurant. She certainly wasn't going to be able to consume any of it.

"Enough stalling. Just get into that shower and get ready before he loses interest—in exhibiting his art collection," she added weakly.

Even she was beginning to realize how flimsy that sounded.

Showering quickly, Leonor freshened her makeup, fussed with her uncooperative hair for exactly three minutes—why couldn't she have been blessed with Jade's straight hair instead of this unruly mass of red waves and curls? she thought accusingly, looking at her reflection—and then got dressed in record time.

The last part was easy. She threw on an emerald-colored sheath dress that brought out her eyes as well as her curves.

Maybe if he looked at that, he wouldn't notice her hair, she thought.

Slipping on a pair of cream-colored high heels, Leonor grabbed her all-purpose shoulder bag and hurried back to the elevator. She had exactly one floor to catch her breath and collect herself.

Good luck with that.

Preoccupied with trying to look nonchalant, she stepped off the elevator car and nearly collided with Josh. He was standing right by the elevator doors, waiting for her.

"Whoa," Josh cried, catching hold of her shoulders to keep her from falling backward from the impact. He flashed her a smile, completely and gallantly glossing over her apparent clumsiness. "Anyone seeing you might think that you were really eager—to eat," he concluded at the last minute.

Nice save, she thought.

She offered him a grateful smile, one that Josh found particularly enticing and strangely compelling, especially given that he wasn't exactly a novice in this area. If anything, he had a problem with women throwing themselves at him. He didn't mind it, but it did get in the way of work.

She went with the excuse he gave her. "I guess I'm hungrier than I thought."

Josh offered her his arm. "Then by all means, let's go," he urged, guiding her toward the revolving door.

The restaurant he took Leonor to specialized in Mexican food, the kind that attracted customers who were raised on that fare and in general avoided restaurants that claimed to offer "genuine" Mexican cuisine because what was offered usually paled in comparison to the actual thing.

But not this time. La Cocina de Mi Madre was the real deal.

Josh waited until after they had been seated and had given their orders to the slightly overworked-looking server before dispensing with what he regarded as small talk that served as merely a "filler."

Taking a sip of the glass of wine he had ordered, Josh put the goblet down. His eyes met hers and he smiled at her like a man who knew something.

"What?" she heard herself asking, her voice sounding just a wee bit uncertain to her own ear.

"I take it this afternoon was a success?" Josh asked. It was obvious he expected her to agree.

But she still wasn't sure just what he was talking about. "Excuse me?"

"When you came back to the B&B this afternoon, you had this satisfied look about you. The kind that said you'd accomplished whatever it was that you set out to do today."

So he *had* been waiting for her—and watching her the whole time she walked across the lobby, she thought. What else did he think he knew? She decided to proceed with caution. It never hurt to be careful.

"I didn't know you dabbled in mind reading."

"I don't," he assured her. "But I do like to study people whenever I can. I find it comes in handy," he explained, "given my chosen field."

"Reading people comes in handy in art?" she questioned. She didn't see the connection.

An uneasy feeling washed over her and had Leonor looking at him more closely.

Once bitten, twice shy, she couldn't help thinking. David had caused her to lose faith in her own judgment as well as in people. It caused her to see red flares, even when they didn't seem likely.

"Absolutely," he told her. "You'd be surprised how many so-called 'legitimate' museums have tried to separate me from my paintings. There are a lot of people waiting to get their hands on valuable art collections so that they can sell them on the black market."

She supposed that being leery of underhanded people went both ways, for a moment seeing things from his perspective.

"Well, I assure you that the museum I represent is most definitely legitimate—as well as very trustworthy," she told him.

"I know," he replied, casually adding, "I checked it out." He saw her eyes widening. "But getting back to you," he went on quickly to distract her, "when you entered the B&B, you looked very pleased with yourself. It was obvious that you were happy with the way something had gone. That's why I asked about this afternoon being a success."

Leonor momentarily debated with herself over the wisdom of making an admission. She supposed that there was no reason *not* to tell him about her sister and the ranch she had. It certainly wasn't any deep, dark secret. Everyone in the area knew about it. And, when she came right down to it, she was proud that Jade had found something to be passionate about. Her youngest sister was doing a service, giving former racehorses shelter while creating a place where children could come and cultivate a love for horses by having firsthand experience with them. Jade also had a few other animals on the small property, hence the word *farm*. Her sister had also created a total experience for the younger set.

Leonor raised her eyes toward his and guilelessly told him, "I guess you inspired me."

It was Josh's turn to be confused. "How's that again?"

"Well, you're going to be sharing some of your art collection with the general public by putting it on display at my museum."

He still didn't see how that could inspire her to do something along those lines. He thought back to the point of his assignment. Was what she was talking about somehow connected to Livia, and if so, how?

"Go on," he urged.

"My younger sister has a ranch where she keeps retired racehorses. They're past their prime but some are perfect for children to ride. A couple of her older horses died a while back, so I brought her a couple to replace them, along with three more. This way, more children can come ride them."

He was still waiting for a useful piece of information to come out of this. If it did, it would most likely wind up incriminating her eventually. This was his job, what he was sent to do and yet… And yet, the idea was making him feel guilty.

He had to be crazy, he told himself. *Just focus, damn it. Focus.*

"And by 'brought' you mean—?"

"I bought them—bargain prices," she added in case he was going to say something about her generosity. She didn't want to dwell on that the same way she didn't want to dwell on the fact that she'd used her money to bail Mac out. She was doing it to help, she thought fiercely, not to get any kind of praise for it. "Like I told my sister, I see this more as a matchmaking arrangement."

"Matchmaking," he repeated, saying it as if it was a foreign word he'd never heard before. That didn't make any sense, he thought. "I'm afraid you lost me."

She looked amused, he realized, and once again found himself captivated by her expression.

"My sister needed some more horses for her ranch and the horses needed an alternative to being put to sleep while they still had so much to offer." She lifted her shoulders in a careless shrug, as if her part in all this was negligible. "I just made it happen."

The woman had a lot of good qualities, he thought. So far, he hadn't been able to find one thing anyone could hold against Leonor.

"She's lucky to have you for a sister," he told her.

"Works both ways," was all Leonor said.

Because he sensed that she wanted to change the subject, he did.

But meanwhile, she had really started him thinking. Maybe this wasn't a self-absorbed puppet who was a junior version of Livia Colton the way some of his superiors believed. Because from everything he had picked up since he had met her, there was a lot more to Leonor Colton than met the eye.

The more he got to know her, the more unlikely it seemed to him that she had been instrumental in her mother's escape.

But he was going to need more than just his gut instincts to go on. Somehow, he was going to have to find proof.

Not to mention that he also needed to find not just who helped Livia escape, but even more important than that, he needed to find the "queenpin" herself.

For now, that meant he was going to have to stick around Leonor a while longer.

He watched as she raised the glass of white wine to her lips and took a sip, her eyes never leaving his.

He'd definitely had worse assignments, Josh thought.

Chapter 10

"You seem a lot happier," Mac observed when she dropped in on him.

It had been almost a week since Leonor had moved out of the small apartment over the stables. Wanting to touch base with Mac, she had come by to see how he was doing.

It was a spur-of-the-moment visit and she had arrived unannounced. As always, Mac was very happy to see her. Leonor might not have had a drop of his blood flowing through her veins but like her sisters, Claudia and Jade, he thought of Leonor as his daughter, in spirit if not in reality.

Mac had been in the corral working with some of his newer horses when he saw her driving up. Calling to his ranch hand to take over, he left the corral and was on the porch by the time Leonor reached the front door of his modest, three-bedroom, single-story home.

Giving her a big hug, Mac invited her inside for a cup of coffee.

"Or we could have it out here, on the porch," he told her, nodded at the swing where they had spent the first few nights when she'd arrived at his ranch, talking until well after midnight.

Not wanting to put Mac to any extra trouble, she'd opted for having coffee in the kitchen.

There was still half a pot left from that morning. Taking it, he was about to pour it out in the sink.

"I can make a fresh pot," he offered.

She was quick to stop him. "No need. It gets stronger the longer you have it on the burner. I like it strong."

"I remember," he told her, pouring her a cup, then one for himself.

They'd sat down at the kitchen table and after a few pleasantries were exchanged he had made his observation about her appearing to be happier now than when she'd first arrived on his doorstep.

"I do?" she asked, hiding behind her cup as she took a long sip.

"Don't play the innocent with me, little girl. I can see right through you," Mac chided with a laugh. "You're happier. I can see it. That wouldn't have anything to do with that art collector your museum boss has you babysitting, would it?" he asked, leaning back in his chair and studying her.

The look on his face told her that Mac already knew the answer to that no matter what she might say to the contrary, so she made no attempt to pretend that she had no idea what he was talking about. But she did deny his perception of the situation.

"I'm not babysitting him, Mac."

"Oh? Then what would you call it?" Mac wanted to know, amused.

She took a long sip of the hot coffee, letting it wind itself through her veins and fortify her before she answered. "I'm showing him around Shadow Creek. And while I'm at it, I'm telling him the advantages of having his collection displayed at my museum."

Mac nodded, taking her words in. And then he asked, "Do you like him?"

She almost choked.

"Mac," Leonor cried. She'd forgotten how very direct Mac could be. He wasn't judgmental; he just didn't waste any words.

Mac was still waiting for an answer from her. "Well, do you?"

She was not about to answer that question. Instead, she gave him an answer she felt they could both live with. "He's a nice man."

It was obviously not enough. "Is he treating you well?"

"Mac, it's not that kind of relationship," she protested.

Mac looked at her in silence for a long moment. "Isn't it?"

She was about to flatly deny it, but then she thought of the other night, when Josh had brought her to her door after they'd gone out to dinner and spent the evening talking about what felt like everything under the sun. For just a moment there, right before she opened the door, she'd thought that he was going to kiss her, and she had to admit she would have let him.

Happily.

But just then, one of the other guests had walked by them, talking loudly on his cell phone and complaining about being late for something. The moment dissipated like a soap bubble in the wind and Josh had backed away, saying that he'd see her bright and early in the morning.

She remembered how frustrated she'd felt, closing the door behind her.

"Not yet, anyway," she finally said.

Mac nodded, as if taking it all in and digesting every nuance, spoken and otherwise. Leaning back in his chair, he look another sip of coffee, then told her, "Jade seems to like him."

She thought maybe she needed to fill in a few details for Mac. "I told Josh about her farm and he said he wanted to see it, so I brought him over there," she explained.

Her words seemed to nudge forward another thought in Mac's mind. "That was a nice thing you did for Jade, buying those Thoroughbreds for her."

Leonor shrugged again. She wasn't comfortable talking about her so-called "good deeds."

"Jade needed them, and they needed her. Seemed like the right thing to do at the time."

He could always read her like a book. "It's okay to own up to doing good deeds, little girl. Nobody's going to think you're bragging. So," he asked, setting down his empty coffee cup on the table in front of him, "when are you going to bring this Joshua around here so I can meet him?"

"Oh, I don't think that's going to happen for a while," she told him.

She didn't want Josh thinking she was attempting to paint him into a corner, or presuming things that hadn't been voiced out loud yet. Whatever was happening between Josh and her—*if* something was happening—was still in a very fragile, unformed state. Rushing it could prove to be fatal to it.

Mac smiled, nodding. "As long as he makes you happy," he said, "that's all that counts."

While it was true that she did feel happy, happier than she had in a long while, she doubted that was what Josh was consciously trying to do. "I don't think that's his primary goal."

Mac wasn't about to argue the point. Some things just *were.* "Still, it's a pretty nice by-product if you ask me," Mac told her.

Leonor visited with Mac a little longer, then drove back to town.

She caught herself humming as she drove.

Mac was right, she admitted to herself. She *was* happier lately, and there was no denying that Josh was responsible for that, whether those were his intentions or not.

Somehow, Josh had managed to penetrate the walls

she had erected around herself, walls that were meant to keep her from being hurt again. Charming, attentive, not to mention so handsome that it almost hurt, Josh had gone from being hard to resist to being absolutely impossible to resist.

Leonor had to admit that she kept waiting for something to go wrong, for Josh to attempt to get something from her, but all he seemed to want was the pleasure of her company.

Could he actually be the genuine article? she couldn't help wondering. Could he actually be as nice, as attentive, as kind as he seemed?

She kept looking for flaws, but try as she might, Leonor couldn't find any. And that in itself had her just a wee bit nervous.

"You're too perfect," she told Josh a couple of evenings later.

As had become their habit these last few weeks, they went out for dinner and this time, he'd found a little club that featured a small band. Catching her completely off guard, Josh had extended his hand to her and asked her to dance.

She hesitated, then gave in. It had been a long time since she'd gone out dancing. Part of her wasn't sure if she even remembered how.

It was a slow number, a song that had been popular several decades ago, and as they swayed to the music, she began to feel that she'd never experienced anything so intimate before. It was as if every part of him was melding with her.

"Excuse me?" Josh asked, thinking he couldn't have heard her correctly.

"You're too perfect," Leonor repeated. "You're kind, you're attentive and you dance as if you've been doing it your whole life."

"I could yell at you, belch, and then step on your feet if you like," he offered innocently. "Would that help?"

He probably thought she was crazy, Leonor told herself.

"Don't mind me," she told Josh with a dismissive laugh. "The last man in my life who treated me well turned out to be a con man and a hustler." Leonor smiled ruefully. "I guess that I'm just waiting for another shoe to drop."

He smiled into her eyes as he continued dancing, all the while feeling the guilt eating away at his stomach lining. In a way, he was behaving like a con man himself. And he was definitely hustling her.

You're not doing it for any kind of personal gain; you're doing it because it's your job.

Somehow, that didn't seem to assuage his conscience. Josh blocked his thoughts, pushing them into the background. "The trick to that," he told her, focusing all of his attention on Leonor, "is to make sure the shoes are both tightly laced," he told her. "That'll keep them from falling."

Leonor looked up at him. Was he warning her, or was she just being paranoid?

Damn you, David. I wish I'd never met you. His shadow seemed to fall over everything.

The music stopped.

"It's getting late," Josh observed. "I can't keep monopolizing you this way. Maybe I should get you back to your suite."

Maybe it would be safer that way after all, she thought, nodding.

"Maybe."

Josh took care of their bill and they left the club. Escorting her back to his vehicle, he released the locks and held the passenger door open for her. Once she was seated, he pulled out the seat belt for her. When she took it, he closed her door and then rounded the trunk to his side of the car.

Getting in, he secured his own belt, and then started up the vehicle.

Definitely too good to be true, Leonor thought. She noticed the concerned expression on his face as he glanced up into the rearview mirror just before he pulled out.

"Something wrong?" she asked him.

"Hmm? No, nothing. Just thinking that guy's following a little too close," he commented. What he didn't say was that he'd noticed that the moment he'd started his car, the driver of the other vehicle had started up his, as well.

He didn't care for coincidences.

Let it go, Josh, he told himself. He'd been overthinking things lately. After a while, everything seemed suspicious to him.

Except for Leonor, which, he knew, was odd in itself. He kept trying to find something on her, and so far, all he could find was that she was a good, decent person who just wanted to reconnect and get along with the members of her family.

Checking into her background had turned up more of the same. She'd kept the bank from foreclosing on the Mackenzie ranch and used her own money to buy those Thoroughbreds for her younger sister's farm. Both came under the heading of good deeds rather than a tit-for-tat arrangement.

If there was a dark side to this woman, he hadn't been able to find it yet.

She talked highly of her mother's foreman, who had taken care of her younger sisters. The man was obviously like a second father to her because he had recently taken her in when she felt the world was closing in on her.

The only person Leonor didn't mention at all was her mother. Not a word. He wondered if that was on purpose, or if it was because she just didn't want to think about the woman.

What could it have been like, growing up and having Livia Colton for a mother? he wondered. There had been no shortage of creature comforts, but there certainly hadn't been any love in her childhood.

Josh found himself feeling sorry for the woman in his passenger seat.

"I'm not perfect, you know," he told her out of the blue.

She was still trying to shake off the effects that had been created when they'd danced together. It took her a moment to realize that he'd just said something. "I'm sorry, what?"

"Back at the club, when we were dancing. You told me that I was too perfect." *If you only knew*, he couldn't help thinking. "But I'm not. I'm not perfect at all."

So far, she hadn't seen anything to contradict her impression. "Let me guess, you use the wrong fork when you eat salad."

"I'm serious," Josh told her, pulling his vehicle into the parking lot.

"Okay, I'll bite. How are you not perfect?" Leonor asked, turning to look at him as she got out.

"Sometimes," Josh said as they walked into the B&B, "I find that my courage fails me."

She strongly doubted that, but maybe they weren't talking about the same thing, Leonor thought.

"You're going to have to give me more of an explanation than that," she told him.

Making their way through the lobby, they went straight to the elevator.

The car was waiting for them, opening its doors the second he pressed the up button.

He'd already said too much and he knew that the more he talked, the greater the likelihood that he would say something to give himself away. But knowing he had to say something, he kept it vague.

"Let's just say that I don't always follow through and do what I really want to do," Josh said vaguely.

That didn't sound like much of a flaw to her, Leonor thought.

Getting off the elevator, they walked to her suite. She used her key and opened her door, then turned toward him.

Her heart was hammering so hard in her throat, she found it difficult to talk.

"And just what is it that you really want to do—but don't?" she asked him in a voice that had mysteriously gone down to just above a whisper.

As it was, her voice sounded very close to husky—and he found it hopelessly seductive.

Standing just inside her suite, Leonor waited for him to answer while her heart continued to imitate the rhythm of a spontaneous drum roll that only grew louder by the moment.

Josh weighed his options for a moment. Damned if he did and damned if he didn't, he couldn't help thinking. And then he answered her.

"Kiss you," he told Leonor, saying the words softly, his breath caressing the skin on her face.

She felt her stomach muscles quickening.

"Maybe you should go ahead and do that," she told him. "I promise I won't stop you."

The drum roll kept growing louder, multiplying to an almost deafening crescendo when he put his arms around her and drew her closer to him.

So close that even a sliver of air couldn't wedge in between their bodies.

It happened in slow motion.

Everything around her faded into a darkening abyss, leaving only the two of them standing within her suite. At the last second, she had the presence of mind to push the door closed.

Somewhere a thousand miles away, she managed to make out the faint *click* of the lock finding its other half, securing itself into place.

And then, as she both saw and *felt* him lowering his mouth to hers, Leonor realized that the earth had come to a complete standstill as a wave of heat rose up and engulfed her.

And then his lips finally touched hers—and set off a wildfire right inside of her chest. At the same time, she could feel this wild, exhilarating rush consuming her, stealing her breath, stealing absolutely everything else and making her feel as if she was suddenly flying, unfettered, along a serpentine path, going down, then up, then down again, blindly following an uncharted course that had been mysteriously carved out by a runaway roller coaster eons ago.

Her heart was pounding so hard, she was sure it was going to burst and all she could do was hang on, winding her arms tightly around Josh's neck, praying that he—and this feeling—wouldn't ever stop.

Chapter 11

He shouldn't be doing this.

The thought echoed over and over again in Josh's brain even as he went on kissing her.

It wasn't that he wasn't attracted to Leonor. If he was really being honest with himself, he was *way* too attracted to her. What bothered him was that this was all happening under false pretenses.

He was lying to her, pretending to be someone he wasn't, and *that* was the person she was doing this with. She was kissing Joshua Pendergrass, billionaire art collector, not Josh Howard, FBI agent.

When he'd started this assignment, he had been convinced that Leonor was the one who had paved the way for her mother's escape from prison. Delving into her finances, he found that Leonor had made a large withdrawal a couple of months ago. He'd been certain the money was to bribe guards to look the other way, as well as to arrange for her mother's getaway once she had gotten beyond prison walls.

But now, given what he'd seen of her generous nature—the bailout for Mackenzie Ranch, the Thoroughbreds she'd bought for her sister and who knows what else she'd financed for her other siblings—Josh was really beginning to doubt that this same woman had anything to do with her mother's escape.

From everything he had learned about her, Leonor Colton was one of the good ones.

Which made what was happening here in her room all wrong.

He didn't want to mislead her, to make love with Leonor under false pretenses. But he knew that if he abruptly stopped, if he found the strength to actually push her away before things went any further, then that would arouse her suspicions and make Leonor begin to suspect that he *wasn't* who he was pretending to be.

He couldn't blow this assignment; there was too much riding on it. Livia Colton was everything that he and countless other people viewed as despicable. She dealt in human trafficking, in drugs and she was a murderer as well as a self-centered, narcissistic sociopath.

She *had* to be caught and stopped.

As for him, damn but he was already caught. Caught and held fast by this feisty redhead with the hypnotic green eyes and the mouth that made him want to sit up and beg.

Deep down in his soul, Josh knew it wasn't right. But he just didn't have it in his power to resist this attraction between them any longer. The best he could do, as they stumbled into her suite and wound up on her king-size bed, their limbs tangled together, was draw his head back just a fraction of an inch and give her one last chance to get away.

There was just enough space between them for him to ask Leonor, "Are you sure?"

Had he given her a bouquet comprised of diamonds, he couldn't have won her heart any more securely. Leonor knew that this man she had already allowed past so many barriers wanted her, could *feel* him wanting her, and yet his first thought was about how *she* felt about this relationship moving forward to the next level.

His thoughtfulness touched her.

Tears came dangerously close to spilling from her eyes as she answered, "Yes," in a low, husky voice.

It was all he needed.

The last barrier was gone, the last stronghold for him to hang on to. Framing Leonor's face with his hands, he kissed her.

Over and over again.

Each time he did, it was more passionate than the last, because each time he kissed her he found himself wanting her more than he had a mere second ago.

He had no idea desire could swell to these proportions.

Still, Josh did his best to resist, to hold off, thinking that at the last moment, her cell phone would ring and she would have to take it, or that someone would knock on her door and it would be one of her siblings, needing her to come with them for some sudden emergency.

But there was no ringing phone, no knock on the door, no one to save Leonor from him at the very last minute.

This overwhelming, burning desire was all there was. A desire that had him peeling away her clothing, covering each newly denuded area with a tapestry of kisses that he wove along her entire, smooth and oh-so-enticing body.

He'd never wanted any woman so much, never wanted anyone to the point of complete distraction like this.

Josh knew that he'd lost not just his way, but all reason, as well. All he wanted was to completely lose himself in her.

There was no beginning, no end, only her.

This was a completely new experience. Leonor had no idea that a heart could pound this hard and still not shatter into a hundred tiny pieces.

He made her feel glorious.

He made her feel ethereal, as if she was one with everything—as long as she could be one with him.

Was this what it felt like to be really, truly in love with someone? Leonor wondered. If it was, then it was wonderful, because she felt totally consumed.

This was *not* her first time—and yet she felt as if it was. As if everything she had ever done or experienced before this very moment was just a poor dress rehearsal, a dry run without the magic, without the exhilarating rush that now just wouldn't stop.

This wasn't like her.

She found herself tugging off his clothes, wanting to touch him, to glide her palms along his lean, hard body and possess him—just the exact same way that he was possessing her.

She didn't recognize herself.

She didn't care.

This was a completely new experience for her and she was thrilled beyond words, totally aware of how lucky she was because something like this came along once in a lifetime.

Maybe.

She only had to compare it to what she had experienced with David. At its pinnacle, lovemaking had been exciting, stirring, but never once did she have to struggle to hold on to her identity, to hold on to her very mind.

Never once had it ever seemed like an out-of-body experience the way it felt right at this moment.

Nude, wanting to arouse him the way he was arousing her, Leonor could only twist and turn beneath his mouth and his hands as shafts of lightning pierced every part of her body.

Josh was doing wondrous things to her, creating a symphony of sensations that until this very moment, she never knew she was capable of feeling.

Never even came close to dreaming it.

When he slowly forged a trail down along her quivering abdomen, deliberately moving ever lower, she bit her lower lip to keep from shouting out as a climax suddenly ripped through her body.

She didn't know which way to turn to capture it and make it last a heartbeat longer.

But she tried.

Exhausted, the sensation slipped seductively away from her body and she finally fell back on the bed, thinking it was over, only to have him re-create the sensation and the moment all over again.

This time, she cried out his name. She could have sworn her body was all but levitating right off the very bed.

With her heart slamming against her rib cage, she struggled to catch her breath.

And then she felt Josh's body sliding along hers. Felt herself priming in anticipation of it joining together with hers.

Astoundingly, it was just getting better and better.

Even with the guilt weighing so heavily on him, every moment he was experiencing with her was better than the last.

And all the while, the anticipation for the final union with her just kept growing.

He was a grown man, not some fourteen-year-old boy eager for his first venture into the world of sexual gratification. He shouldn't be feeling this way.

And yet, there was no denying that he was.

And it was wonderful.

It felt like nothing else in the world mattered but this moment, this woman.

This sensation that had seized him, refusing to let him go.

Lacing his hands through hers, his eyes seeing only hers, Joshua moved her legs gently apart. And then, as he saw her catch and hold her breath, he entered her.

The next second, he felt Leonor breathe faster as her body yielded to his.

The moment they became one, he initiated another dance, one that was totally different, completely more gratifying than the one they had shared on the floor of that little club what now seemed like a hundred years ago.

The rhythm increased with every passing second.

They moved faster and faster until it was all one wild blur of a whirlwind, a race during which they held on to one another tightly as they went up the ethereal mountain that beckoned to them.

And once scaled, once they'd reached the very peak, there was only one way left open to them.

Leonor cried out his name, the sound muffled against his lips. She could actually *taste* his response.

Dizzy, she clung to Josh, wishing with all her heart that this euphoria that had taken possession of her would never fade.

Knowing all the while that it had to.

But she clung to him anyway. And reveled in the feel of his arms around her, the pressure of his body on top of hers.

The euphoria slid away far more quickly than he thought it would. The weight of his guilt was responsible for that. It had managed to deftly pierce the protective bubble that the aftermath of lovemaking had left behind in its wake.

Josh let out a shaky breath, doing his best to pull his wits together. Fervently hoping that she wouldn't hate him once she found out who he was.

Rolling off Leonor, he asked, "I didn't hurt you, did I?"

"No, why?" She turned her head to look at him. "Did I wince?"

She was teasing. She didn't expect him to take her question seriously. But the expression on his face told her that he did.

The joyful haze she was clinging to was in serious jeopardy of breaking up like the mist on the horizon at dawn.

"No, but I thought that maybe I was too rough."

He honestly didn't know what had come over him. He'd never just dived off the deep end that way before. Never lost track of everything except for the woman in his arms before. It was a totally incredible experience for him—but it was the consequences of all that which had him worried now.

"Too rough?" Leonor echoed, totally mystified. That wasn't rough; that was superb. "No, you were perfect." Her words echoed back to her and she could feel her cheeks growing hot. "I know I'm not supposed to say something like that, but you were. I felt…wonderful," she finally said, after mentally discarding half a dozen words trying to find the right one to describe the light show that was *still* going on inside of her.

Once she said it, once she had given voice to "wonderful," she knew that there wasn't any other word that even came close to depicting what was going on inside of her.

It was like having captured sunshine in a bottle, she thought.

She wanted to embrace the whole world. But she would "settle" for embracing him.

Shifting so that she fit against the hollow that his body formed, Leonor lightly brushed her lips against his neck, moving ever so slowly toward his throat.

Possessing every fraction of an inch that she came in contact with.

"Leonor, what are you doing?" Each word was a struggle to get out. Even his breathing had become labored. She was setting him on fire again.

How was that possible?

He would have sworn that there wasn't anything left inside of him to rise to the occasion. But somehow, incredibly, there was.

"If you have to ask, then I'm doing this all wrong," she murmured, her breath seductively warming his skin with each syllable.

He could feel himself getting aroused and hard all over again. Wanting her all over again.

The weight of his guilt slowly beginning to dissipate again even as he silently lectured himself to get a grip.

His lecture, admittedly halfhearted, fell on deaf ears.

Trying to exercise some sort of control over himself, Josh propped up on his elbow and looked down into her face. He could feel his heart swelling.

"You're not tired?" he asked.

Her smile was at once seductive and amazingly innocent.

"On the contrary, I'm invigorated," she told him. A sultry laugh punctuated her words. Leonor slid her body in such a way that it was practically beneath his. "Want to find something to do?" she asked, a wicked grin curving her lips.

He was already sliding his hand possessively along the swell of her hips, caressing her. Reclaiming her. "What did you have in mind?"

She moved her face closer to his and breathed, "Guess."

Laughter mingled with desire as he asked, "If I guess right, will you promise to share your vitamins with me? Because I swear you're going to wind up wearing me out, woman."

"I think you underestimate yourself," she told him, moving her head just enough to capture his lips and press hers against them.

"Well, I certainly underestimated you," he murmured against her mouth a beat before he silenced her lips with his own.

It began again, that rush, that desire, that wild,

exhilarating roller-coaster ride that she had already experienced once tonight.

This time the impact was even greater, more all consuming.

Even with David, there hadn't been this overwhelming craving, this desire to take and be taken, to make love and be made love to over and over again until there wasn't a single breath left in her body.

Or his.

She didn't know exactly when she'd undergone this incredible transformation; she only knew that Josh was responsible for it. Even though slivers of fear still lurked in the recesses of her mind, fear that Josh would somehow betray her and break her heart the same way that David had, Leonor ardently blocked it from her consciousness.

Dwelling instead on the wonderful way this man that fate and her own museum director had caused to cross her path made her feel.

They made love a total of three times that night and each time seemed even more fulfilling than the last because each time they did it, a sense of caring enveloped them.

As she drifted off to sleep, an incredible, seductive sense of contentment slowly slid through her veins.

If this *was* too good to be true—if *he* was too good to be true—then she didn't want to wake up tomorrow, Leonor thought. Having experienced the perfect moment, she knew she couldn't possibly hope for anything better, anything more.

But being human, she did.

* * *

He couldn't sleep. Exhausted as hell, Josh still couldn't sleep. So he finally disentangled himself from Leonor, intending to slip out of her bed and go to his own room.

Josh felt like a man trapped in a deception with no way out.

But that same feeling was why he decided to remain just where he was, at least for tonight. Because he knew that this could be the last time he would be with her like this.

So for tonight, he contented himself with watching Leonor sleep, wishing with all his heart that he hadn't barged into her life like this. Wishing that somehow, their paths had crossed without an assignment attached to it.

Wishing with all his heart that he didn't feel the way he did.

Because falling for an assignment was definitely frowned upon by the department, he thought.

He was a man trapped between the proverbial rock and a hard place. He couldn't tell her who he was and he couldn't *not* tell her. Even if by some magical act of fate, Livia Colton turned up right here in the middle of the night and he captured her, that would change nothing between Leonor and him and he knew it.

Rock and a hard place, he thought again with a sigh.

Josh continued to watch Leonor as she went on sleeping, praying daylight would never come.

Chapter 12

Leonor stirred. Stretching, she slowly opened her eyes. The next moment, she swallowed a small cry of surprise.

Josh was in bed beside her, but that wasn't why she'd almost cried out. Instead of being asleep, he had his head propped up on the palm of his hand and he was leaning on his elbow, watching her.

He looked as if he had been watching her for a long time.

Gathering herself together, Leonor asked a little uncertainly, "Have you been watching me like that all night?" She wasn't quite sure what to make of having someone just observing her sleep like this.

"Pretty much," Josh admitted. And then he shrugged carelessly. "I had trouble sleeping."

Having Livia Colton as a mother had done a number on her confidence. In moments of weakness, she tended to take on blame. "I'm sorry, did I keep you awake? Was I tossing from side to side?"

He shook his head ever so slightly, just the tiniest hint of a smile touching his lips.

"Actually, you sleep very still. I kept checking to see if you were breathing." He hadn't really, but he grasped at the excuse, thinking she might find it acceptable as to what was really keeping him awake like this.

"Well, I guess it's better than snoring," she commented, still feeling a little self-conscious about waking up to find Josh just staring at her. "Maybe you'll sleep better in your own room."

His smile grew a little wider. "Are you kicking me out?" Josh asked, amused.

"No," she cried, not wanting him to misunderstand and think that she had absolutely *any* regrets about what had happened between them last night. "I was just thinking that maybe you would sleep better alone—a lot of people do, from what I've read," she interjected. "Besides, you can't go a whole night without sleep. You'll feel like a zombie if you do that."

She was concerned about him—and he was spying on her. His guilt just kept getting larger and larger as it gnawed away at him, he thought ruefully.

"I'll be fine," he assured her. "Haven't you heard of pulling an all-nighter?"

The smile crept across her lips slowly, curving the

corners of her mouth as it went. He found it hopelessly seductive—and told himself not to.

"We nearly did," Leonor pointed out.

He needed to clear his head—before he gave in and made love with her again, guilt or no guilt.

"Tell you what," he suggested briskly, "let me grab a quick change of clothes and I'll meet you in the lobby, say in about half an hour, and we'll go out for breakfast."

"Make it an hour. I need to freshen up," she told him. Leonor sat up, pulling the sheet up with her.

"No, you don't," Josh contradicted. He was trying very hard just to look at her face and not the sagging sheet that was revealing far more than it hid. "You look perfect just the way you are."

"An hour," she emphasized with an amused smile.

"An hour," he agreed.

Giving her a quick kiss—anything more and he knew he was *not* going to leave—Josh scooped up his clothes and hurriedly got dressed.

He was doing his best to avoid eye contact, but he could still feel her eyes on him.

"You know," he told Leonor, "it's not polite to stare."

"Oh, was I staring?" she asked in an innocent voice that wouldn't have fooled a two-year-old. "I wasn't aware that I was doing that."

"You were," he assured her with a knowing look.

"I'll just have to try to get that under control," she told him.

He stole another quick kiss. Damn, but he wanted her, he thought, struggling with himself.

"You do that," he told her just before he left her suite.

Leonor slid back down in the bed, content to absorb what was left of the heat that Josh's body had generated and left behind.

She was in no hurry to get up. At least, not yet.

Josh's room was located on the floor above Leonor's. Rather than wait for the elevator, he went to the stairs and took them two at a time.

He entered this room just in time to hear his cell phone ringing, the one he *didn't* take with him when he was with Leonor.

He didn't have to look at the screen to know who was calling.

"Any progress?" the deep voice on the other end ground out without any preamble.

Josh sat down on the bed before answering. "I'm beginning to think that we were all wrong about Livia's oldest daughter."

"Oh?" The tone told him that his boss was *not* of like mind.

"I don't think that Leonor Colton had anything to do with her mother's prison escape and frankly—" he paused for a moment, wondering if he was making a mistake, telling Arroyo this "I'm not feeling too good about this deception."

As he could have predicted, his superior was *not* sympathetic.

"Well, suck it up, Howard. If I wanted a choirboy for this assignment, I would have brought one in. Your job is to nail this woman and get her to tell you where her mother's holed up. And spend as little money as you can doing it," he tossed in as a reminder.

That had sounded all well and good on paper, but now that he had gotten to know Leonor, he wasn't so sure anymore. "What if Leonor Colton doesn't know where she is?"

"She knows," Arroyo assured him confidently. "This kind of thing doesn't happen in a vacuum. Now get back in there and find out what the woman knows. That's an order, Howard."

And with that, Arroyo abruptly terminated the call.

Josh curbed the sudden temptation to throw the cell phone across the room. But breaking it and temporarily disabling his communications with Arroyo wouldn't solve anything. He put it back into the rear of the third dresser drawer, then covered it with his socks and underwear.

Showering quickly, he dressed and was downstairs in the lobby in under the hour that they had agreed on.

So was Leonor.

She surprised him.

She was sitting in one of the chairs in the lobby, waiting for him. Her red hair was loose about her shoulders and he could have sworn that, like a siren song, it was calling to him, coaxing him to slip his fingers in and pull her to him so he could kiss her.

Get a grip, he ordered.

"You're ready," he noted, walking up to her.

He watched her smile bloom across her face. "You sound surprised."

He inclined his head, conceding the point. "Most women, when they say an hour, usually mean at least an hour and a half. Maybe two."

Her eyes met his. "I'm not most women," Leonor told him.

He looked at her and for a moment, the teasing humor was gone, replaced by something that felt suspiciously like affection.

"Yes," he said, "I know."

Damn, there went her heart, Leonor thought.

Don't get carried away, Lennie. Just because the man knows how to set fire to the sheets doesn't mean that you're suddenly going to be plighting your troth to one another in the near future. C'mon, stay real, stay focused.

But it was really hard to focus on anything other than Josh, feeling the way she did right now. It was as if her feet were just barely making contact with the ground as she walked. Any second, she was liable to be floating on air.

"In the mood for something different?" Josh asked her.

She pressed her lips together, keeping the almost-giddy laughter from slipping out. "I thought that was what last night was about."

He was the one who laughed then, captivated by the unassuming way she had about her.

"No, I'm talking about breakfast," he said.

"Unless it includes fried rattlesnake, I'm open to it," she told him gamely. So far, his choice of restaurants hadn't disappointed her.

"Good, because I know this quaint little hole-in-the-wall that serves the best breakfast burritos," he told her, gesturing toward the B&B's back door. "We could actually walk to it, but I think we might want to ride on the way back. These things are so good, people have a tendency to eat more than they should," he warned her.

He turned around just in time to see it out of the corner of his eye. An unremarkable silver vehicle, not unlike countless others in the area. Except that this one was going rather fast.

And from the looks of it, it was headed straight for Leonor.

Quick reflexes honed with years of practice had him reacting automatically. He made a dive for Leonor and, bringing her down, he covered her with his body before she even fully realized just what was happening or that she was in danger.

The silver sedan wound up missing her by less than six inches. The driver never slowed down; he just kept right on going.

Josh quickly scrambled to his feet, reaching for the weapon he usually carried—the one that, just like the other cell phone, wasn't there. He'd taken his service weapon and stored it in his vehicle, afraid that if Leonor saw it on him, it might make her suspicious.

The next second, time froze. His attention was completely centered on the woman he'd just saved. Nothing else mattered.

He looked her over as quickly as he could. To his relief, he didn't see any blood.

Yet. That didn't mean that she hadn't been hit.

"Are you all right?" he asked Leonor.

"I am, thanks to you," she answered, accepting the hand he offered her. Feeling shaken, she rose to her feet and brushed herself off. "I think you just saved me from becoming that guy's hood ornament." Trying to regain control over her shaky feelings, she blew out a breath. "Thank you," she said in earnest.

"I'm just glad I was here." He looked at her, concerned. "Are you sure you're all right? No broken bones, no bruises—anything?" he asked tactfully, looking her over one more time.

She moved her shoulders, and then took a couple of steps forward. "No, everything seems to be in working order."

"Hey, are you two all right?" the handyman from the B&B called out as he ran up to them. "I saw the whole thing. That driver was crazy, man! He had all that space and he almost mowed you down. You want me to call the police?" he offered, lowering his voice slightly.

Leonor immediately vetoed the idea. "No, nobody was hurt and that guy's long gone."

"I got the license plate!" the handyman announced proudly, looking at Josh. "Maybe the police can track the driver down."

"No, that's okay," Leonor told him.

The last thing she wanted was the kind of publicity that this sort of an incident generated. She knew it would only cause the people in town to begin speculating about her and her family all over again. And then the rumors, old and unfounded, would begin again. She'd had enough of that to last a lifetime and was just beginning to enjoy the fact that it had finally died down. She didn't need a new eruption.

"Why don't you give it to me, just in case?" Josh told the handyman.

"Sure." The man was more than happy to comply. He pulled out a small pad and wrote the license plate number down. Tearing off the page, he handed it to Josh.

Josh looked at it before he folded the paper. There was a fifty-fifty chance the car had been stolen or that different plates had been put on, but in case it hadn't been, maybe he could get someone in the department to trace it back to the owner. This way, he could get a handle on who was trying to kill Leonor—because the driver definitely hadn't been heading for him.

This near hit-and-run added a whole new twist to the case, he thought.

As he pocketed the paper with the license written on it, he saw Leonor looking at him strangely. It made him uneasy. *Had* she been hurt?

"You want to go back into the bed-and-breakfast?" he asked, thinking that maybe it was best for her if she lay down and rested after something like this.

But Leonor wasn't thinking about resting. "No, but I would like to know why you just pocketed that idiot's license."

"Because walking around holding the paper is kind of awkward," he answered flippantly.

Leonor frowned. "That's not what I meant and you know it."

Maybe she just needed reassurance, he thought. After all, she had just been through an ordeal that would have reduced another woman to tears, or worse, hysteria. So he gave her as straight an answer as he could.

"I just want to hang on to it in case something else happens. This way we might have a lead for the police to follow up on." She was still looking at him rather oddly, forcing him to ask, "What?"

"Who are you?" she wanted to know.

Did she suspect? His stomach tightened for just a fraction of a moment before he got himself under control and answered, "Someone who wants to make sure that you're kept safe."

But she shook her head. That wasn't what she was asking. "Besides that."

Josh knew he had no option open but to brazen his way through this. He told himself his cover hadn't been blown. He was too good at what he did for that to have happened.

Right, that's why you made love with her last night until the cows came home.

The expression was something his grandmother used to say. The memory, coming out of the blue the way it did, rattled him.

It took him a second more to answer. "You know who I am. Your boss apparently vetted me. I'm the guy you've been after to share his art collection with you, remember?"

She didn't address that. Instead, she focused on the one thing that was somehow bothering her—the one thing that had, ironically, saved her. "Your reflexes are very quick."

His gut told him where this was headed. "I have a trainer. I also know how to drive defensively," he told her, getting ahead of what she might ask next. "It's something rich people either learn how to do or hire someone to do for them because sooner or later, a kidnapper is going to pop up in their lives and if they're not ready for him, then it's all over."

She shivered, as if coming out of a trance. "I'm sorry," she apologized. "You saved my life and I'm grilling you."

"You're rattled and you have every right to be," he told her soothingly, then asked again, "You sure you don't want to go back to your room? We could order room service."

She shook her head. "No, I just want to go somewhere, get this out of my system," she told him. She sounded agitated.

"Then let's go," he urged, opening the passenger door for her and waiting for her to get in.

He was being exceedingly nice, as well as thoughtful, not to mention that he'd just saved her, and she was acting as if she suspected him of doing something awful, Leonor upbraided herself.

She really *was* getting paranoid, she thought.

Leonor got into the vehicle and had buckled up by the time Josh rounded the hood and got in on his side. But rather than buckle up, he paused and looked at her face closely.

She shifted self-consciously. All those years with photographers snapping away at her and she still felt self-conscious.

"What's the matter? Did my makeup get wiped off?"

"No, I'm just checking you for scratches—but it's just as I suspected," he told her.

"What?" she wanted to know.

"You're perfect," he told her, and then he lost the serious look and a grin came out. "Possibly even more perfect than before."

She shook her head and laughed. He was good for her, she thought, feeling ashamed that just for a moment, she had begun to suspect him. Once burned, twice shy; wasn't that how that old adage went?

"Just drive," she told him, pointing to the road in front of their windshield.

"I hear and obey," he answered with just enough whimsy in his voice to keep her fooled.

Or so he hoped.

Chapter 13

"Your hunch was right, Josh," Jeremy Bailey, the computer tech he'd called at the San Antonio field office, told him later that afternoon. Even with a rush order, it had taken Bailey four hours to get back to him. "The license number you gave me belongs to a car that was reported stolen over a week ago. Sorry I don't have any better news."

Josh sighed. This was one of those times he would have preferred *not* being right.

"Not your fault," he told Bailey.

This meant that he was back to square one, Josh thought, trying not to let that get to him. But after coming up against one dead end after another, it was getting progressively more difficult for him to remain upbeat.

He'd gone into this thinking that Leonor was the mastermind behind her mother's escape, or at least one of them. He no longer thought that. Now it was beginning to look to him as if her mother was trying to eliminate Leonor. But it was just a hunch and he needed to find a way to prove that.

"So what are you going to do?" Bailey asked him, curious. They were not only colleagues, they were friends when time allowed.

"Same thing I've been doing all along—play it by ear," Josh said, then added, "Except that now I also need to keep Leonor Colton out of harm's way."

"Good luck with that," the computer tech told him before terminating the connection.

Josh's next order of business was to report in to Arroyo and give his superior a quick update, emphasis on the word *quick*.

Or at least that was his plan. But Arroyo had a battery of questions.

"Sounds like there's trouble in paradise," Arroyo commented after he heard Josh out.

Josh wasn't sure if the assistant director was referring to the fledgling relationship he was attempting to build with Leonor in order to gain her trust, or if Arroyo was talking about the state of the supposed relationship between Leonor and Livia.

Deciding to stay on the safe side and not read anything into the man's words, Josh played dumb and asked, "How so?"

Arroyo huffed. "Any fool can see that the girl got

Mama Bear angry and now Mama Bear's looking to get rid of what she considers to be another loose end."

Meaning Leonor, Josh thought. Wanting to make sure that he and the assistant director were on the same page, he felt Arroyo out a little further.

"What you're saying is that Livia Colton hired someone to kill her daughter."

"Hell, yes," Arroyo cried. "From everything I've heard, in comparison to the Colton matriarch, Lizzie Borden was a warm, nurturing pussycat."

Josh knew that by no stretch of the imagination could the word *loving* be applied to Livia Colton, but he was beginning to harbor some doubts that she would actually have her own flesh and blood killed.

"Still," Josh theorized, "going from cold, unapproachable witch to murderous mother is a pretty big leap."

"Not so big," Arroyo countered. "The woman's a sociopath. But if you think that you've got a better theory, let's hear it," he urged.

Josh paused, reviewing the facts of the case in his mind. "Well, to be honest, I think you might be right in thinking that Leonor's mother is trying to kill her—"

"So we're on the same page," Arroyo declared, obviously pleased that his senior agent was agreeing with him.

Josh cut in before Arroyo could continue. "But we disagree as to why Livia's trying to get rid of her oldest daughter."

He heard Arroyo's stifled exasperated sigh. The

man was close to uttering some very choice words but he refrained—for now. “Go ahead.”

“I think that Livia’s out for revenge because Leonor *didn’t* help her. The woman somehow still managed to pull off an escape and now she’s out to get even with everyone who might have turned their back on her.”

Arroyo didn’t even pause to reflect on his agent’s theory. “So, in other words, you think that witch is out to get all her kids?”

Although as far as he knew, there hadn’t been any attempts made on any of the other Coltons yet, Josh had a feeling that it was only a matter of time. Right now, Leonor was apparently the first on her mother’s hit list.

“Why not?” Josh said. “Livia Colton belongs to the old ‘if you’re not with me, you’re against me’ school of thought.”

“You’re probably right,” Arroyo conceded. “But *somebody* had to have helped that witch escape and it’s a matter of record that Leonor was the only one of Livia’s kids who came to visit her.”

“What can I tell you?” The phrase slipped out before he realized he’d said it. Josh braced himself for fallout as he added, “Leonor Colton’s got a soft heart.”

“I don’t care if she’s a walking bowl of mush. In my book, that woman’s guilty until *proven* innocent.” And then Arroyo remembered a damning piece of evidence. “What about that big chunk of money Leonor withdrew a few months ago? Those prison guards were bribed to look the other way and

Livia's getaway was clean, going off without a hitch. That all costs big bucks."

"I'm aware of that, but the money had to come from somewhere else. Leonor used *her* money to keep her mother's old foreman from losing his ranch and she also just bought several Thoroughbreds for her sister Jade's farm after a couple of the original horses she had there died."

Arroyo blew out a disgusted sigh. "And at Christmas time she flies around in a sled, distributing toys to all the good little girls and boys and going, 'Ho, ho, ho,'" the assistant director mocked.

Taking offense on Leonor's behalf, Josh was barely holding on to his temper, but he knew he couldn't afford to lose it. Arroyo would have him removed in a heartbeat and he could do Leonor more good right where he was.

"I couldn't speak to that, sir," he managed to say calmly. "I can only speak to what I can personally verify."

Irritated, Arroyo said, "Yeah, yeah, just keep your eyes open. I want that woman's hide nailed to the barn door."

He wasn't 100 percent certain that the assistant director was talking about the escaped fugitive. "You are talking about Livia Colton, right, sir?"

Arroyo sighed. "She's the main target, yeah. If you can find her—and exonerate your girlfriend while you're at it—then by all means, go for it."

Josh felt he needed to correct the assistant director, just for the record. "She's not my girlfriend, sir."

"Yeah, well I'm not a hundred percent convinced of that, Special Agent Howard. And in case it's slipped your mind with all this wining and dining you've been doing," Arroyo said sarcastically, "the brass wants to see results."

That brought something else to mind. "Speaking of results, sir, the museum that Leonor works for is waiting for those paintings I'm supposedly 'loaning' to them to arrive."

"Well, then I guess you'd better hurry and wrap this thing up," Arroyo snapped.

Josh could envision the whole thing blowing up on him. He'd already caught Leonor looking at him oddly a couple of times since the near hit-and-run incident. He knew something was bothering her and he definitely didn't want to arouse her suspicions any further.

"I thought the head of the department had an arrangement going with the real owner of those paintings that I showed to Leonor."

If the sigh coming from Arroyo had been any louder, Josh had a feeling it would have blown out his ear. He sounded far from happy as he said, "I'll see what can be done."

"Good." Josh leveled with him. "Because I don't think I can keep stalling them much longer."

Arroyo laughed drily. "From where I'm standing, I think you're a master at it. I'll get back to you," he told Josh, and then the connection went dead.

Josh frowned at his phone. This was definitely *not* going well.

* * *

Leonor was conflicted. On the one hand, Joshua Pendergrass was just as perfect as she'd said he was. Everything a woman could wish for—and more. He was kind, considerate, handsome, rich and an absolutely incredible lover.

Added to that, he was heroic.

That was the word for it. *Heroic.* Had he not acted so quickly, she might be currently looking at life from a hospital bed, at least for the immediate future.

And yet it was that very act of heroism that disturbed her.

Yes, it was perfectly plausible that Josh had just reacted instinctively when that car came barreling straight at her—he did tell her that he'd taken lessons in defending himself and in being proactive when it came to his own protection.

There was no denying that she was lucky he'd been there that morning.

But there was just *something* about that whole thing that disturbed her.

She couldn't put her finger on it, but it felt like he was behaving more like a bodyguard than a billionaire who knew how to defend himself. Thanks to the world her mother had created, she'd been around both bodyguards and rich people for most of her life, and she could distinguish between the two. Comparing them, she felt that Joshua behaved as if he belonged to the former category rather than the latter.

When she thought about it, there were certain things he did that reminded her of her older brother,

Knox. Knox was a Texas Ranger, a man sworn to defend the defenseless. Or River, she thought suddenly. River was a Marine.

She was just being paranoid, Leonor upbraided herself, annoyed. Burned by David, there was no question that she was afraid that Josh was going to somehow turn out to be just like him in some way.

Maybe it was because she'd fallen so hard for Josh that she was really worried that the bottom was going to drop out and that this time she would wind up being hurt beyond repair.

She was overthinking this again, Leonor told herself.

What she needed was a distraction, some sort of project. She was due back at the museum in less than a week for the gala that was being thrown to highlight both the paintings from Josh's collection as well as from several other collectors, but that did leave her with time on her hands until then. Josh had made some excuse about needing to "take care of some business," which, at the moment, left her to her own devices.

She knew that she could go back to Jade and visit with her, but visiting was not *doing* and she really needed to be doing something, distracting herself before she possibly wound up blowing the best thing that had ever happened to her.

If it was the best thing that had ever happened to her, she qualified nervously.

Like an answer to a prayer, her sister Claudia picked that exact moment to call, telling Leonor that she'd breezed back into town from New York and subsequently into her sister's life.

Her timing couldn't have been more perfect—even though Leonor thought that there seemed to be something a little "off" about Claudia's manner on the phone.

Claudia's parentage was even more offbeat than the rest of the Colton siblings. Younger than Thorne and older than Jade, Claudia had supposedly been conceived while Livia was touring France. Livia claimed that while there, getting over her divorce from River's father, she'd married a Frenchman named Claude after a wild, whirlwind courtship. That marriage ended in divorce just as her other marriages had, and Livia returned to the States with a new baby daughter she'd named Claudia.

Because this was Livia, no one around her even blinked an eye.

Different from the others in her own way, from the time she was a little girl, Claudia had always had a keen sense of fashion. There was no disputing that from a very young age, she was the personification of glamour down to her very toes.

Fresh from her success in the fashion industry in New York City, Claudia had declared that, ready or not, she intended to bring her designs to Shadow Creek.

"I want to open up a boutique right here," Claudia told Leonor as they shared a lunch at one of the restaurants that Josh had taken her to. "A boutique that sells clothes to real women, not just the toothpicks you see in fashion magazines."

"You mean in Shadow Creek?" Leonor questioned. She would have thought her sister would have wanted a more urban venue. Shadow Creek's very name made it sound small-town and rural, as though it was struggling to make its way in the twenty-first century.

Claudia lifted her shoulders in a careless shrug. "Sure, why not? It's called progress, Leonor. There's no reason why Shadow Creek can't become just as urban as Dallas and Houston. Or even New York City," she concluded. "The transformation has to start somewhere, right?" she asked Leonor with a small, whimsical laugh that sounded strangely hollow to Leonor's ear.

Leonor looked at her closely. "You're serious?" she questioned because Claudia had been known to change her mind in the middle of a project and just turn her attention to something else entirely.

Of course, Claudia had been younger then, but still it didn't hurt to be certain of her younger sister's intentions before she gave Claudia her backing.

"Of course I'm serious," Claudia told her with enthusiasm. "Why wouldn't I be?"

"No reason."

That wasn't quite accurate because Leonor felt she was getting the same sort of subtle signals from Claudia that she'd sensed from Josh.

Maybe she was just overreacting. She needed to calm down, take a breath and just accept things at face value, she silently counseled. Especially when it came to helping her siblings.

"Okay," she said after a beat, "if you're really serious about this, then I think it's wonderful." Looking at Claudia for a long moment, she asked, "Would you like a partner?"

"Well, to be completely honest, I can't do it alone," Claudia admitted. "I just don't have enough capital available for that."

"I thought you were doing well in New York," Leonor said.

"I was."

Leonor didn't understand. Had her sister gone through all that money? And if so, how? "Then what's the problem?"

"The problem is that I was under contract with Designs Original and I had to buy out my contract if I wanted to leave. So I did. But that left me short on working capital. So, to answer your question again, yes, I'd like a partner, but it depends on who that partner is," she qualified.

Leonor waited a moment before saying, "Me."

"You?" Claudia repeated, her eyes widening in disbelief. This was so out of Leonor's field. "*You* want to be my partner in the fashion industry?"

"That's what I'm suggesting," Leonor told her. She waited for a formal answer from Claudia now that her sister knew that she would be the one who she would be going into partnership with.

"Yes!" Claudia cried excitedly, her eyes sparkling. "Hell, yes!" she added for good measure. Overjoyed and a little dazed—she hadn't expected Leonor to make her this offer—she asked, "So when do we get started?"

"Well, I thought now would be a good time," Leonor answered, watching her sister's expression closely for any indication that she suddenly wanted to back out. "I saw this old building on Main Street the other day that might just be perfect for what you had in mind."

It was Claudia's turn to nervously ask, "Are you sure?"

Leonor never hesitated. "Very," she responded.

Abandoning her chair, Claudia hurried around the small table for two and threw her arms around her older sister's neck. "Oh, Leonor, you're a godsend!"

"Well, that's certainly better than some of the other things I've been called in the last month."

Claudia looked at her quizzically as she loosened her arms from around her sister's neck. And then it suddenly dawned on her what Leonor was referring to. Her mouth all but fell open.

"You're talking about that awful blog, aren't you?" Claudia guessed.

Leonor nodded. Though she hated the subject with a passion, she knew she might as well clear the air now, before they went forward. She wanted Claudia to know the truth so she wouldn't be swayed by any lies that she might hear later.

"I said some things to someone I trusted—someone I thought I loved, actually." In hindsight, she realized that she really *didn't* love David. She certainly didn't feel about him the way she felt about Josh. "And it turned out that he was only with me to pump information out of me about Mother and the rest of us. He couldn't *wait* to sell what I'd told him in confidence to that online *rag*." She spat out that word, using an old-fashioned term that once described a publication that dealt in sensationalism and fabrication for its own sake.

"You don't owe me any explanations, Leonor. We've all been there," Claudia assured her sister, sounding like someone who had encountered her own set of betrayals in her time.

"Okay, now that we've cleared the air, let's go and scout out that property on Main Street to see if it's right for your purposes," Leonor told her sister, although she was rather confident that Claudia would like it.

Getting up, Leonor took out a large bill that more than covered their lunches as well as a very generous tip and placed it over the check the server had left on the table.

She was glad to be able to focus on something outside of herself and the thoughts that kept insisting on plaguing her.

Excited and looking forward to opening her business in what had been her home town, Claudia enthused, "You're the best!" as they headed toward the restaurant's front door.

"At least I'll do until 'the best' comes along," Leonor told Claudia with a small laugh.

She was only half kidding.

Chapter 14

"So, what do you think?" Leonor asked two hours later as she, Claudia and Amanda Smith, the Realtor showing them the property, came out of the small, two-story abandoned building on Main Street. Although it had formerly been a warehouse, it seemed perfect for Claudia's new boutique.

The real estate agent showing them the property paused to lock up before joining the two women.

Claudia had toured the building twice, just to be sure.

"Well, it needs some work," Claudia speculated. "But I think we can put the creative offices upstairs and downstairs, we can have the showroom for the customers to see the finished designs." Making up her mind, Claudia grinned at her big sister, her eyes sparkling. "I think this just might be happening."

"Wonderful," Amanda declared, pleased that the sale had been this easy. "I'll get in contact with the owner and see if the three of you can come to terms about the sale price," she told the two women. She walked across the street with them to where her vehicle and theirs were parked along the curb.

"I'll get back to you within the hour," the Realtor promised. She got into her car and waved at Claudia and Leonor.

"I really can't thank you enough, Leonor," Claudia said to her sister. Opening the door on the passenger side, she started to get into Leonor's vehicle. She was already busy making plans for the ground floor layout in her head.

About to tell her that there was no need for thanks, Leonor's voice was drowned out by the sound of an engine being gunned. The loud noise was accompanied by squealing tires. Without thinking, she instinctively turned toward the sound.

For the second time in as many days, Leonor was startled to see a vehicle flying toward her, going far faster than the speed limit.

Just as the sight registered, she felt her arm being grabbed from the side and the next moment, she was being unceremoniously yanked out of harm's way.

Watching all this unfold, Claudia shrieked in fear for her sister's safety.

The driver of the vehicle, a tan Nissan this time, sped away, leaving only a blur in his wake.

Stunned, her heart was hammering wildly in her throat where it had lodged when she'd been pulled out of harm's way.

For the second time in as many days, she'd managed to cheat death.

It took Leonor a moment to realize that she'd been saved—again—by the man she had been spending most of her time with these last few of weeks.

It felt like déjà vu.

How was this possible? she silently demanded in confusion. Although she was exceedingly grateful, it seemed like too much of a coincidence.

"Josh?" she gasped in disbelief. "Where did you come from?"

"He just saved your life, Leonor," Claudia cried, stumbling out of Leonor's car. "The least you can do is thank the man." It was obvious by her expression that she was wondering who the heroic man was.

Josh barely took notice of the other woman emerging out of Leonor's car. His attention was focused exclusively on Leonor.

"Are you all right?" he wanted to know. Wanting to make sure himself, Josh held on to her shoulders as he looked her up and down, carefully assessing every inch of her for any damage.

It was a lucky thing he had decided to keep an eye on her, even when she went out with her sister. He'd had a feeling that Livia wasn't the type to stop after only one attempt, which meant that Leonor's life was still in danger.

"I don't know," Leonor answered honestly.

Shaken, she looked down at herself, then at the skid marks on the ground next to her vehicle. Skid marks that had come dangerously close to her and would have definitely make fatal contact if Josh hadn't been there to pull her out of the way.

"Yes," she finally managed to say.

Just then, as Leonor turned, the sun hit something at waist level, causing it to momentarily shine and catch her attention. When she looked down to see what it was, she spotted the gun tucked into the front of Josh's waistband. The weapon would have been hidden by his jacket, but when he grabbed her, the fabric moved and the gun became exposed.

For the second time in two minutes, she caught her breath.

Her eyes widened as she looked up at the man who had saved her not once, but twice—or had that been orchestrated for some reason?

She was no longer sure of anything.

"You have a gun," Leonor said numbly.

Damn, he'd meant to be more careful. But something had told him that he might need the weapon today. And when he saw that car speeding at her, all he could think of was saving Leonor. Not Leonor, his assignment, but Leonor, the woman he had made love with.

"I have a license for it," he told her in a deliberate calm voice. "I use it for protection."

Glancing over her shoulder to make sure that the

crazed driver wasn't suddenly about to make a reappearance, Claudia crossed over to the driver's side where her sister and the man who had saved her life were standing.

"Leonor, who is this man?" she asked, waiting for an introduction.

Leonor looked up at Josh. "I don't know," she replied numbly.

He was 80 percent certain that his cover was blown, but even so, Josh did his best to exercise as much damage control as he could. Maybe this wasn't a total loss, he told himself. At least he certainly hoped that it wasn't.

"Yes you do," he told Leonor. "I'm the same man you've been spending the last few weeks with." His tone grew very serious. "After that last incident yesterday, I thought I should keep an eye on you and make sure you were safe." Turning toward her sister—he'd recognized Claudia from the photo in his file, but he pretended otherwise—Josh extended his hand to the blonde and said pleasantly, "I'm Joshua Pendergrass. Your sister and I have been discussing the possibility of exhibiting part of my art collection at the museum where she works."

The young woman happily grasped Josh's hand and shook it with feeling. "Well, I'm certainly glad she knows you." Claudia looked at her older sister. "You didn't tell me about Mr. Pendergrass—"

"Josh, please," Josh insisted, hoping that if he was nice to her sister, Leonor would get past the fact that he had a habit of turning up unexpectedly.

But he had little hope of that. Leonor was looking at him as if he was the one behind these hit-and-run incidents instead of the real perpetrator.

"You didn't tell me about Josh," Claudia said, accepting the correction as she looked at her sister over her shoulder. Turning back to Josh, her eyes skimmed over him from top to toe, obviously assessing the man. Her smile showed she definitely approved of what she saw.

Still feeling numb as well as shaken, Leonor answered quietly, "No, I didn't."

"Wait," Claudia suddenly cried, replaying what Josh had said before introducing himself to her. "Did you just say that someone tried to run her over before this?"

Josh never looked away from Leonor. Did she have any idea how serious this situation really was, or was she in denial?

"Yes," he said, answering her sister's question.

Horrified, Claudia shifted toward her older sister. "Leonor, is someone trying to kill you?" she demanded in disbelief. The next moment she cried, "Who?"

Leonor waved her hand at her sister's question, refusing to consider that idea. "It was just a coincidence."

Rather than taking Leonor's word for it—she knew her sister had a habit of downplaying things—Claudia looked at the man who had just risked his life to save Leonor's. It was obvious that she thought she'd get a truthful answer from him.

"Is it?" she asked him.

Instead of saying yes or no outright, Josh turned his attention to Leonor and told her, "I think you should report this to the police."

There wasn't a hint of a smile to be had. He hoped that by telling her to go to the police, he'd divert Leonor's attention away from the fact that he had been tailing her.

"Why?" she wanted to know, a tinge of sarcasm in her voice. "After all, I have you to come to my rescue," she pointed out.

She felt like her heart was cracking right in half. Josh—if that was actually his name—was lying to her, she thought. She could *feel* it. She had stupidly disregarded all her own carefully constructed warnings and allowed herself to fall for this man. To take this man to her bed, make love with him, and by doing so, she'd started building castles in the air—castles with absolutely no foundations beneath them.

Castles that were bound to come back down to earth with a resounding crash.

What did it take for her to learn that she couldn't just believe in happy endings because they didn't happen to people like her?

Leonor blinked hard, struggling to keep the tears back. She refused to let him see her cry. She *refused* to cry over the likes of him.

She could feel the moisture forming.

Grasping her by her shoulders, as if that could somehow help his words penetrate, he said, "Leonor, this is serious. Someone is trying to kill you. Do you understand?"

Claudia stifled a cry. Hearing the words out loud made everything seem that much worse. There was genuine concern in her eyes as she looked to her sister for an answer. "Leonor?"

"It's just a stupid coincidence, that's all," she told Claudia.

She wasn't thinking about the near hit-and-runs; she'd survived those. She was thinking about the fact that she'd been lied to—again—and that she just might *not* survive.

Her heart was literally aching in her chest. All she wanted to do was run and get away from him. But somehow, she remained where she was, as if her feet were glued to the ground.

Josh had an answer for Claudia. "Your mother," he told her flatly.

"Livia?" Claudia cried, appalled as well as stunned. It was obvious that the information made no sense to her. "Why?"

"No reason. It's just his imagination," Leonor answered, dismissing what Josh had just said. She felt literally sick to her stomach.

But Josh wasn't ready to retreat yet. He was determined to make his point. "That blog spilling all the family secrets is why she'd be after Leonor," Josh said, answering Claudia's question. "Somehow she found out that Leonor was the one who gave that blogger's source all the information."

Leonor raised her chin stubbornly. "My mother

would never hurt me," she insisted. "And certainly not for something like that," she added.

But Claudia wasn't so sure. "Maybe he's right, Leonor. I mean the rest of us have forgiven you and moved on, but Livia's not like the rest of us," Claudia reminded her.

"No, she's not," Leonor agreed, but that was just her point. "Everyone in the family was angry because you thought I sold you out—" she began, laying out her argument.

"Well, I wasn't really angry, just upset," Claudia admitted, cutting in. "But not for long," she quickly added.

"But Livia is very vain," Leonor doggedly continued, sparing Josh the barest of glances. "She absolutely *adores* publicity. The more, the better. There's nothing she loves more than to have her story all over the news."

She looked at Claudia pointedly. All her life Claudia had insisted she felt like the outsider in the family, but even an outsider was able to notice things if the pattern kept being repeated.

"I think we can all agree that the woman really wants to be infamous and that article certainly painted her that way," Leonor concluded.

"If your mother isn't trying to kill you, then who is?" he wanted to know.

Leonor raised her shoulders in a vague shrug. "I haven't got the slightest idea," she told him. "But then, I don't seem to know anything about anyone." She looked at him pointedly as if to drive her point home.

Claudia shifted, unclear as to what was going on between her older sister and the handsome man who had come rushing to her aid.

She looked from Leonor to the man who, in her opinion, had heroically saved her sister's life—maybe twice, according to him.

"Is this a lover's quarrel?" she finally asked uncertainly.

"No!" Leonor cried with a little too much feeling.

Rather than make any comment on whether or not love in any form was involved, Josh said, "It's not a quarrel. At best," he added, looking at Leonor's hardened profile, "it's a misunderstanding."

"Right," Leonor said, her eyes narrowing to almost-angry slits. "And apparently I misunderstood you all the way around."

"We need to talk," he informed Leonor. Not waiting for her response, he turned toward Claudia and said, "Can I call you a cab? Or drop you off somewhere?"

Claudia resourcefully came up with an idea. "My car's parked by the restaurant where Leonor and I ate earlier. Why don't I drive her car there, get my car and leave hers in the parking lot? This way, you and she can have some privacy," she suggested.

"I don't want any privacy with him," Leonor insisted, speaking up.

Claudia gave her a reproving look, then pulled her sister aside to talk to her.

"Lennie, you're my big sister and I love you and I mean this in the most loving way—don't be so pigheaded. That man just risked his life saving yours and one look at his face tells me that he definitely has feelings for you. I'm thinking that you've got a real chance at happiness here, despite the family curse—"

Confused, Leonor repeated, "Family curse?"

"Mother," Claudia explained, biting off the word as if it was poisonous and needed to be spat out before it had a deadly effect. "Now give me your car keys," she hissed into Leonor's ear, "and for heaven's sakes, listen to what he has to say."

But Leonor wasn't about to be so easily swayed. "The last time I listened to what someone who professed to have my 'best' interests at heart had to say," she told Claudia, "he fooled me into trusting him with family secrets, and then he wound up conning me out of a million dollars before he took off. I don't need to go through an experience like David Marshall again."

But Claudia wasn't convinced that lightning was about to strike twice. "You really think he's going to do that?" she asked, nodding at Josh.

Leonor was not about to give up her stand easily. "Well, maybe he won't get any money—but that's only because I've got it locked up in a trust that only I can access under certain provisions," she added.

Claudia looked unconvinced. "Is that the only reason you think he won't try to con you and get your money?" her sister challenged.

Leonor wanted to remain steadfast—but she was losing ground and she knew it. Even her heart was turning against her, hoping against hope that she was wrong somehow.

"Probably not," she murmured quietly.

Claudia glanced again at Josh. She wasn't the world's best judge of character, but there was just something about this man that made her believe he had Leonor's best interests at heart.

"Look, all I ask is that you give him a chance to explain before you dump him. Sounds fair, doesn't it?" she asked.

"'Fair' has nothing to do with it." Leonor began to work herself up again. "How do I know he won't give me some sob story, try to con me that way?"

"How do you know that what he's telling you *isn't* the truth?" Claudia challenged.

Leonor stared at her younger sister. The one she had just bankrolled to restart her career in Shadow Creek. "Why are you on his side?" she wanted to know.

"I'm not on his side," she protested. "I'm on yours. And you need someone," Claudia insisted. "From what I can see, I think that he's it. Now, I can't tell you what to do—"

"Ha!"

Claudia relented. "Okay, I can try, but you're the final authority here and you know it. I just think it'd be a shame to slam the door on something before you explore all the possibilities that 'something' has to offer." She glanced around Leonor's shoulder to look at Josh again. "Especially when those possibilities come in a package that is so damn *cute*," she said with feeling and no small appreciation.

Leonor sighed, temporarily surrendering. Digging

into her pocket, she took out her car keys and handed them to Claudia.

"Fine. Here."

Claudia happily closed her hand around the keys. "Great. I'll leave them for you with the hostess at the restaurant," she told her.

Hurrying to Leonor's car, she got in the driver's side. She buckled up and started the vehicle. Looking at Josh, Claudia waved and said, "Good luck," before she drove away.

Thinking it was safe to rejoin her, Josh walked over to Leonor and asked, "Ready to go?"

Leonor gritted her teeth together and ground out, "No."

He was flexible. Right now, he had to be. "We can stay here and talk for a while if you want," he offered. "I don't think that driver'll be back."

When he mentioned the person who had almost mowed her down, she remembered something. "I didn't thank you for saving me," she said grudgingly.

The smile rose slowly to his lips, a little like the sun making its first appearance on the horizon. "No, you didn't," he agreed.

"Thank you," Leonor mumbled less than willingly.

He held the car door open for her and waited until she got in.

"Anytime, Leonor," he told her as he closed and secured the passenger door. "Anytime at all."

Chapter 15

With all her heart, Leonor wished she could just take off somewhere, cutting herself off from everyone and everything just long enough to be able to try to pull herself together. She wanted to get her bearings and be able to move forward with her life.

But she didn't have the luxury of indulging herself that way. She had to get back to Austin and back to the museum.

Oh, she supposed that she could just hand in her resignation, but her sense of responsibility wouldn't allow her to do that. Sheffield had made it clear more than once that he depended on her and if she quit, that would be leaving him in the lurch at the worst possible time. It wasn't as if he could just pull another curator out of a hat, and the museum *was* scheduled to hold that huge gala opening for the new works of art that had been acquired.

Works of art that did *not* include any paintings from "Joshua Pendergrass's" private collection, because she sincerely doubted that there *was* actually a private collection to speak of.

Leonor moved around the suite, throwing things into her suitcases as she packed.

She had tried to pin Josh down about the paintings right after he had saved her life. She'd felt conflicted pressing him for answers after he'd been so heroic, but then, for all she knew, he might have had someone make it *look* as if they were trying to run her down just so that he could play the hero. This way she would be grateful to him and consequently feel as if she was in his debt.

Leonor dropped the makeup she was packing on the floor. Swallowing an oath—she kept dropping things because she was trying to hurry and leave before Josh knocked on her door—Leonor bent down to pick up the tiny containers. Tossing them haphazardly into one of the suitcases, she stopped for a moment and took a deep breath.

Get a grip, Lennie!

She didn't know what kind of game Josh was playing; all she knew was that she didn't want to play games. She'd been played once by David and this had all the earmarks of another con.

A unique one, but still another con.

This was why she'd decided to check out this morning. She was going back to Austin and the museum where hopefully, with any luck, she would forget all about Josh.

In about a hundred years or so, Leonor thought ruefully.

When had she become so pessimistic, she upbraided herself.

Less dawdling, more moving, Leonor silently ordered.

She looked around the suite one final time. Satisfied that she hadn't left anything behind, she closed the lids on both suitcases and snapped the locks into place.

Time to go.

With a suitcase in each hand and a bag slung over her shoulder, Leonor made her way to the suite's door. Opening it, she exhaled. She was making a clean getaway.

Almost.

The moment she stepped out of her suite, she found herself, suitcases and all, walking smack into Josh. She very nearly had all the air knocked out of her.

"Whoa." He laughed, catching her by the shoulders. A big, warm smile graced his lips. "They told me at the front desk you were checking out."

Determined to leave, Leonor avoided his eyes, giving her answer to the space next to him. "I am. I did. I've got to get back to work."

"At the museum?" he questioned, moving to take her suitcases from her.

Leonor deliberately shifted them away, out of his reach. She didn't want him touching her suitcases, or her. She just wanted to get away from Josh as fast as she could.

"That is none of your business," she said between clenched teeth.

He wasn't an idiot. He knew something was wrong, but he went on as if it wasn't, hoping to gloss over the rough patches and eventually get her to let him back into her life.

"But I thought we were in negotiations to have my art collection displayed at the museum," he said, "mystified" by her sudden change of plans.

This time Leonor *did* look up at him and her eyes were nothing short of blazing. "Drop the act, Josh, or whatever your real name is," she snapped. She was tired of being played for a fool.

"It is Josh," he told her in a calm voice.

She jumped on his words, putting her own interpretation to them. "Then you admit that the rest of what you told me was all an act."

The triumph of being right felt very hollow to her and she took no comfort in it.

"We can talk about that later," Josh began, trying to take the suitcases again.

She pulled away for a second time. "*No,* we can't," Leonor retorted, sidestepping him. She intended to take the stairs, determined to get away from him as fast as possible. "Now get out of my way!"

His voice was as calm as hers was sharp. "Not going to happen."

Josh put his hand up against the wall right in front of her, blocking her exit.

Furious, Leonor glared at him. She knew that if she pivoted and went in the opposite direction, he would still get in front of her and stop her, so she didn't even bother trying.

"Someone is out to get you, Leonor," he told her in the same maddeningly calm voice, "and I'm not going to let them hurt you."

Her chin shot up defiantly. "How do I know that's not you?" she challenged. "How do I know that *you're* not the one who's out to hurt me?"

"Because I'm not," he told her. "You're just going to have to trust me."

Just like David. "Right, because you're so trustworthy," Leonor shot back.

He ignored the sarcasm. "Actually," he told her, "I am."

How could he possibly say that? Just how simple-minded did he think she was? For a second, Leonor was so angry she couldn't even speak. When she finally did find her voice, it was to accuse him.

"You lied to me!"

He wasn't going to insult her by denying it. "Just to get close to you."

She hadn't expected him to admit it that readily. At a loss for words, she shouted, "Go to hell!" and then darted past him—or tried to.

"Most likely," he allowed, "but not yet. First I need to find out who's trying to kill you. Once they're in prison, *then* I'll see about getting those hotter accommodations."

Did he think he was being funny? She was so

angry at him, she could hardly think. "I can call the sheriff," she threatened.

"But you won't," he said with confidence that she found infuriating. And then he told her why, showing her that he knew her better than she knew herself. "You've had enough of that kind of attention to last you a lifetime and you're not about to willingly invite that back into your life if you can help it."

She wanted to pound on Josh with her fists, but she knew he'd hardly feel it. "What do you *want* from me?" Leonor demanded.

"Nothing," he told her. His voice was so mild, to the general passerby it would have sounded as if they were having a general conversation—unless they took note of the tension pulsing between them. "I just want to keep you safe."

Because of Livia, she had come to painfully learn that everyone had a motive. He had to have a motive for his suggestion.

"Why?" she demanded.

He looked at her for a long moment, debating saying something offhanded in response. But that wouldn't do here. So he put himself on the line and told her the truth.

"Because," he said, his eyes meeting hers, "heaven help me, something happened between us in your room. Now I'm not the world's brightest man, but I'm smart enough to know that kind of thing doesn't happen between two people very often—"

"What? Having sex?" she asked sarcastically. "I hear it happens all the time."

When he spoke, his voice was low, intense, going to her very core. "It was more than just that and you know it."

The sigh Leonor blew out was long and ragged. She couldn't argue with him because she knew he was right and she knew that he knew. But she was not about to let him back into her life until she had at least some of her questions answered.

"I am not taking another step with you until you tell me who you really are."

Josh knew she was serious.

He carefully weighed his options, trying to decide if there was any possible way he could avoid answering her question and still get her to let him accompany her. He knew he could fabricate something—he'd been in tighter situations than this. But none of those situations had held the life of someone he really cared about in the balance.

He was good at his job, good at being able to walk into a room and see all the possible ways someone could either break in or make an escape. There wasn't anyone he felt he could entrust Leonor's safety to outside of himself.

And she wouldn't allow him into her life until she had the truth.

"Finish checking out," he told her. "And then come for a ride with me." He saw the leery, guarded look that immediately entered her eyes. "Please," he added, then offered her what he knew she'd been waiting for. "I'll tell you everything you want to know then."

It was her turn to examine her options. “How do I know you’re not going to try to kidnap me?”

He laughed drily. “If I was going to do that, I would have done it long before now. I had the opportunity,” he reminded her.

She knew he was talking about when they’d made love in her suite. She certainly hadn’t been in any position to offer resistance.

Inclining her head, she gave in—sort of. “All right, but we’ll go for a drive in *my* car.”

He nodded. “No problem.”

She had one final condition. “And I drive,” she told him.

He looked as if he had been expecting her to say that. “Fine.”

Leonor still couldn’t help thinking that she was going to regret this. Josh was taller and a great deal stronger than she was. She knew he could easily overpower her and if it came down to that, she really had nothing to defend herself with.

But there was a part of her that *wanted* to trust him and that part knew that if she turned her back on all this, if she stormed away without hearing him out, she would wind up regretting it. Maybe not now or even very soon, but eventually—and very possibly for the rest of her life.

She capitulated.

“All right,” she told Josh stiffly, “let’s go. And believe me, this had better be good.”

“I don’t know how ‘good’ you’re going to think it

is," Josh told her honestly. "But I promise it *will* be the truth."

Still frustrated, Leonor momentarily surrendered. "I guess I can't ask for more than that."

He knew a lot of women who could. He was grateful that she wasn't among them.

Josh pressed for the elevator.

They got out on the ground floor a moment later and she proceeded to the registration desk to check out. Josh did the same.

Leonor kept one eye on him throughout the entire procedure and he was well aware of it. He couldn't really say that he blamed her. But he fervently hoped that by the time he was finished explaining things to her, she would understand why he had lied to her. Understand and eventually forgive him because he didn't think he could come to terms with living in a world without her being a part of it. Without being a part of his life.

Once they checked out, Leonor had the attendant bring her car around.

"And yours, sir?" the attendant asked Josh once he brought out her vehicle.

"I'll have someone make arrangements for it later," he told the man, giving him a tip to cover both. The attendant was grinning broadly as he tucked it away in his pocket.

Leonor put her suitcases into the trunk of her car, then closed it. Keeping the vehicle between them, she made her way to the driver's side and got in. She watched Josh's every move as he got in on the passenger side. Her eyes never left him as she buckled up.

"You realize you're going to have to look at the road once you start up the car," Josh pointed out, mild amusement curving his generous mouth.

She was in no mood for his humor. "You let me worry about the road. You just worry about you," she informed him sharply.

He really couldn't blame Leonor for looking at him like that, but she was making him a little uneasy because her attention was so divided. She was ripe for an accident.

"I've got an idea," he suggested.

"What?" she bit off.

"Why don't you pull over to the shoulder of the road so you can keep an eye on me while I tell you what you want to know?" He could see that she was still suspicious of every word coming out of his mouth. "I just wanted to be able to talk to you someplace where we wouldn't be overheard."

Saying something unintelligible under her breath, Leonor made a sharp right and pulled over the way he had suggested.

Turning off the engine, she removed the key from the ignition, closing her hand over it. He took that as a sign that she still didn't trust him. For now, he knew he had to accept that.

"All right, I'm listening." She saw him move his hand toward his pocket and immediately became alert. "What are you doing?"

"Reaching for my wallet," he told her. "I want to

show you my ID. My *real* ID," he emphasized before she could ask about it. Withdrawing it slowly from his pocket, he flipped open his wallet. "I'm an FBI agent. Special Agent Josh Howard," he said, introducing himself even though it said so on his photo ID.

"I see," she said numbly. The FBI. This was even worse than she had thought. Someone had told him to spy on her. Why? She wasn't important in the scheme of things. "And I'm what?" she demanded. "Your assignment?"

"Actually," Josh corrected, "your mother is. I just assumed, after I saw those bank withdrawals that you made, that you were my best shot at finding where Livia Colton was."

In a matter of seconds, it all became clear. Leonor put two and two together. "You thought I bribed the guards."

"It looked that way," he admitted. "But after checking into things further, I know what you used the money for."

She resented him looking into her finances, even though apparently doing that had exonerated her. "So now you *don't* think I helped Livia escape." She waited for him to walk back his words, or come up with something equally as infuriating to her.

But he didn't. "No, I don't," he told her.

"All right." She'd go along with that, although she wasn't 100 percent convinced he was telling her the truth. "So if you don't think I got her out of jail, what are you still doing here?"

"I told you," he said patiently. "Trying to protect

you. You might not have had anything to do with your mother's prison escape, but someone *is* after you." He laid his cards on the table, at least for this aspect of the case. "You don't seem to think it's your mother. I'm not convinced that it isn't, but either way, someone *is* after you and I intend to find out who it is, and then put them away for it."

It sounded so simple when he said it that way. Simple and gallant. She didn't want to be won over. Struggling to hold on to her anger, she gave him a penetrating look. "And that's it?"

He spread his hands wide, the way someone who had nothing to hide, nothing up his sleeve, might. "Yes, that's it."

"And I'm just supposed to believe you?" she challenged. She couldn't shake her feelings of frustration, hurt and confusion.

"Well," Josh began philosophically, "I just blew my cover and very possibly put my ten-year career with the department in jeopardy, so yes, I'm asking you to believe me." Pausing for a moment, he went for broke. "And I'm also asking you to let me go back to Austin with you, to that gala."

The man had an incredible amount of gall; she'd give him that. "What am I supposed to tell Sheffield? You don't have an art collection and he's not exactly going to get all excited about some fake copies you're going to try to pass off as the real thing if that's what you have in mind."

He supposed he couldn't blame her for feeling that

way. "Don't worry," he reassured her. "The Bureau is not run by amateurs."

What was *that* supposed to mean? She took a stab interpreting his words. "There *are* paintings?"

He nodded and responded in a mild voice, "There are paintings."

Her eyes widened. Did he mean what she thought he meant? "The ones in the photographs you showed me the other day?"

"The very same." He could see that Leonor was still exceedingly skeptical about what he was telling her. "The head of my department is friends with the real collector and the collector graciously agreed to lend out his paintings—after all the proper documents were signed and the insurance company was assured that the proper precautions would be taken." He smiled at her. "The paintings are being lent to an upscale art museum, not to a crime syndicate. Your boss will be none the wiser."

"He's also hoping for a sizable donation from you to the museum," she reminded him.

"Well, there he might be a little disappointed," Josh admitted. "But who knows, when all this is finally over, the real collector might be persuaded to make some sort of donation to the museum."

She wasn't taking a single word for granted. She wanted it all spelled out. "And by 'finally over' you mean—?"

He obliged her by playing along and making things clear. "Your mother returned to prison and whoever is after you taken down."

Right, like that was going to happen. He had no idea who he was dealing with if he thought that Livia could be brought in just like that. Livia might have been taken once, but that was *not* going to happen again, except over her mother's dead body. He had to know that, Leonor thought.

"So," she sighed, "in other words, never."

"You need to have more faith than that," he told Leonor.

And then, suddenly leaning over toward her, Josh allowed himself just one quick kiss, brushing his lips against hers. It succeeded in vividly bringing back the other night in all its glory. And made him want things he wasn't about to put into words at the moment.

"I know I do," he told her.

The look in her eyes when she raised them to his told him that maybe she would get there.

Eventually.

Chapter 16

Adam Sheffield seemed to light up like an airport runway turned on for a plane landing in the dead of night the moment he saw his curator entering the art museum with Joshua Pendergrass. While talking to several members of the museum crew, he stopped in midsentence and made straight for Leonor and her companion.

After one quick, welcoming smile thrown in Leonor's direction, the silver-haired, well-dressed museum director focused his entire attention on the man she had brought in with her.

"Mr. Sheffield," Leonor began, "This is—" She got no further.

"No introductions are necessary," Sheffield told her effusively. As luck would have it, they were standing right in front of the paintings that had been loaned to the museum in Josh's name. Sheffield caught up Josh's hand in both of his and held it fast. "I can't tell you how excited we are to have these wonderful paintings on display here in our humble little museum."

Josh spared him just the barest of distant smiles, indicating that they were both aware that the museum they were in was neither little nor humble and that he knew that Sheffield was only attempting to play the part of a self-effacing museum director.

"It's my pleasure, Mr. Sheffield," he told the older man.

"Call me Adam, please," Sheffield instructed, baring two rows of gleaming white teeth that would have made any cosmetic dentist beam with pride.

"Well, Adam," Josh continued obligingly, "I only have one request."

"Name it," Sheffield instantly responded with marked enthusiasm.

"This plaque you have beside the paintings—" Josh began, pointing to the one that had been hung up just this morning in preparation for the gala. It cited that the paintings were on loan from his private art collection. His name was written in rather large letters.

"Not big enough?" Sheffield guessed. "I can have them make a bigger one. It'll be touch and go getting it done before tomorrow's gala, but I'm sure that it can be arranged—"

Josh raised his voice in order to stop the onslaught of words coming from the director. "No! I would rather you just had the word *Anonymous* written on it instead of my name."

Sheffield looked at him blankly for a moment. He dealt in a world filled with a great many inflated egos. But then the director managed to collect himself. "Now you're being much too modest, Mr. Pendergrass," Sheffield chided with a laugh.

"Call it a quirk," Josh allowed. "But I would rather that my name didn't get around."

Sheffield looked completely bewildered by the request. "But why—?"

Before Josh could come up with an excuse, Leonor came to his rescue by telling her boss, "If his name is made public, Mr. Pendergrass feels that he might be bombarded with appeals and requests from other museums and galleries. He'd rather be in a position to pick and choose just who he allows to display his collections rather than have to deal with all those annoying requests."

"Oh, I see." Sheffield nodded his head several times. He grew solemn for a moment before saying, "I get it. Of course, I do think you should get some credit for this, but I totally understand you wanting to stay out of the spotlight. Of *course* we can remove the plaque and have it changed to Anonymous. Consider it done!" Sheffield declared obsequiously. He looked at the younger man almost shyly as he asked, "But you will come to the gala, won't you?"

Josh glanced at the woman at his side, then smiled broadly at the director. "I wouldn't miss it for the world, Adam."

"Splendid!" Sheffield enthused. He turned his attention toward his curator for a moment. "You did an excellent job, Leonor, recruiting Mr. Pendergrass's paintings for us." He fairly beamed at her. He obviously wanted to cull Pendergrass's favor further and said to Leonor, "Why don't you take the rest of today off and show Mr. Pendergrass around our fair city?"

She was about to protest that the very reason she had come back today was to help prepare things for tomorrow's reopening and gala, but she decided to go along with Sheffield's suggestion. Not because she wanted to show Josh around Austin—she had a feeling that the man knew his way around the city just fine—but because she could use the time to pay a visit to her half brother, Robert, her late father's son, and his family. It had been a long time since she'd seen any of them and she was feeling particularly nostalgic about reconnecting to her past.

So she inclined her head, acquiescing, and replied, "Very good, Mr. Sheffield."

"I'm game," Josh announced, slipping his arm around her as he ushered Leonor toward the exit. Lowering his voice, he told her, "That was pretty quick back there. I have to say that I was impressed."

"By what, exactly?" she asked. She'd done her best not to stiffen when he put his arm around her, but now that they had cleared the room and left Sheffield behind, she immediately shrugged off his arm.

"Your explanation to your boss about why I didn't want my name posted on that plaque next to those paintings."

She walked next to Josh as they left the museum and went out into the street. "I'm assuming that you didn't want to have art experts coming after you, brandishing torches and pitchforks once they realized the paintings were fakes."

"They're not fakes," he corrected mildly. "They're the real thing."

Leonor stopped walking and looked at him incredulously, wondering if he was being truthful. She *wanted* him to be, but at the same time she was afraid of getting burned. "You're serious."

He made an elaborate cross over his heart, as if that was enough to bear him out. "Completely. I told you the department would come through."

She didn't understand, then. "If they're real, then what's the big deal about not having you identified as the donor whose collection those paintings came from?"

"Because," he explained patiently, "I'm not the donor and if he can't have the credit—because it would jeopardize the operation if he did—then I don't think it's right to have my name up there so that I steal his thunder."

Leonor shook her head. "You are a strange man, Joshua 'Pendergrass.'"

He smiled because she had remembered to use his alias even though he had told her his real surname. "I prefer the word *complicated* to *strange*," Josh replied whimsically.

"Well, I call them as I see them," Leonor replied only to hear him laugh.

She really wished she didn't find herself responding to that sound, and she *really* wished that she could completely divorce herself from reacting to Josh in any way.

But that wasn't about to happen, especially since, at least until the gala was over, she was going to have to interact with him for almost the entire time. Sheffield had all but told her to babysit the man.

So, for at least the next forty-eight hours, she was stuck.

"So, what 'sights' are you going to show me?" Josh asked gamely as he led her over to his car.

She frowned. "I'm sure that there's nothing here that you haven't seen before," she told him.

As he stopped by his vehicle, Josh's eyes swept over her body languidly and with a familiarity that had her feeling almost itchy. She was still angry at him—so why did she want him so much?

"True," Josh agreed. "But I certainly wouldn't mind seeing some things again."

His meaning immediately hit her and Leonor could feel herself reddening even as she desperately tried not to react.

"I was talking about Austin," she said between clenched teeth.

"Oh." His smile widened as he allowed himself to think back to the other night in her suite. "I wasn't."

"Yes, I figured that part out," she informed him curtly.

"Anyway," he continued as if there was no tension

building on her side, "where would you like to take me?" He opened the passenger door for her.

Leonor pushed it shut with a quick movement of her wrist. "Nowhere. I'm going to visit my half brother."

She saw the change in him immediately, even though he tried to bury it. He was alert and on his guard. "Which one?"

She frowned. "It's none of the ones that you know," she informed him coolly. "My late father had a son years before he ever made the mistake of crossing Livia's path. Once she sank her hooks into him, that poor old man never stood a chance. She dazzled him, got him to marry her and less than a year later, he died, leaving half his fortune to me with Livia as the executor. I hear that my brother, RJ, contested the revised will, but he eventually lost. Livia had excellent lawyers." She raised her chin defiantly. "Not exactly your typical 'and they lived happily ever after' story."

She had that right, Josh thought. There was only one question in his mind. "And you want to visit this half brother why?"

"Because RJ is family," she said simply. And family was becoming increasingly important to her. "He's almost old enough to be my father, when you come right down to it," she admitted. "But he doesn't hold the fact that Livia managed to have my father sign over half of his fortune to me against me."

Josh's eyes met hers, pinning her down. "You're sure about that?"

Her chin rose a little higher as she told him, "Yes, I am."

Josh nodded agreeably as he took in the information. Maybe a little *too* agreeably. "Then you won't mind if I tag along."

"Actually," she told him, tired of politely dancing around the way she really felt just to come off as being agreeable, "I do."

He flashed her a smile as he opened the passenger door for her again. "I'll pretend I didn't hear that."

She sighed wearily. It didn't seem worth arguing over. "So you're going to come with me no matter what I say?"

His smile only grew wider. "That's the general idea."

She got into the car. He was quick to get in on the driver's side.

"Isn't this considered harassment?" Leonor challenged.

"No—" he started up his car "—it's considered making sure you remain alive."

A small, annoyed noise escaped her lips. "I didn't know that that was part of your assignment."

He shrugged. "Sometimes I improvise as I go along," Josh told her.

"And there's nothing I can say to make you change your mind?" she wanted to know. Part of her felt hemmed in—the other part felt, heaven help her, protected.

"Oh, sure," he answered.

She blinked. Was he telling her the truth? "And that is?"

"'Let's go spend the day in your room' would do it," he told her, sparing her a quick glance and winking before he turned back to watch the road.

Leonor rolled her eyes and sighed, pretending to be exasperated.

Okay, so maybe the scenario he had just proposed was not without its appeal. But the last thing she needed was to act on his suggestion, no matter how much the idea tempted her.

The night they had spent together was still very fresh in her mind. Fresh enough to bring all the yearning back big-time, and in her present state of mind, she wasn't up to dealing with all that as well as everything else that was currently on her plate—not the least of which was a fugitive mother who was the closest thing to a crime kingpin she knew.

"I'll just call my brother to tell him that I'm bringing someone," Leonor said with a sigh, taking out her cell phone.

Even though he was driving, one hand whipped out and he caught her wrist to keep her from tapping out her brother's number on the keypad.

She glared at him. "Just what do you think you're doing?" she demanded.

He released her wrist. "For simplicity's sake, you might as well just introduce me as someone lending some of his art collection to the museum."

They were back to that cover story, were they? "You want me to lie to RJ?"

His tone was mild when he answered her. "I want you to keep your stories straight in case your brother shows up at the museum gala—you are thinking of inviting him, aren't you?" he guessed.

Sheffield was inviting well-connected people, CEOs of big companies and the like, all in hopes of generating more revenue for the museum.

"My brother runs my late father's company, so yes, the thought had crossed my mind." She was stalling, heaven only knew why. Her brother and his wife and children already had their invitations. "All right, I see your point," Leonor said, relenting. For a brief, shining moment, she had entertained the thought of just being honest with RJ but that obviously wasn't going to work here. "You're Joshua Pendergrass, big-time—and modest—art collector. Happy?"

He smiled at her as he pulled away from the curb and onto the through street. "Happy," he told her. "Now, what's your brother's home address?"

RJ Hartman, his wife, Madeline, and his three adult children lived in a large, two-story, 4,200 square foot house just outside of Austin. While it was apparent that Leonor's half brother did not have the kind of money that Livia had at the pinnacle of her criminal reign, Josh noted that there appeared to be no resentment toward Leonor from either her older brother or his wife, both of whom greeted Leonor warmly and were exceedingly polite toward him, as well.

As the visit wore on, Madeline Hartman insisted that they stay for lunch.

"Just a few things I've thrown together," she told them.

Madeline, it turned out, had "thrown together" a three-course meal that also included appetizers and a dessert that Leonor told her sister-in-law was simply "to die for."

"*You* should visit more often," Madeline told her, obviously pleased by the compliment as she set another, extra-large slice of wine cake on her plate.

"So tell me more about this gala your museum is holding," RJ encouraged as the four of them, plus two of their three children, sat in the dining room, making short work of Madeline's wine cake.

"I'm really hoping that you'll be there," Leonor said. "It's only being held tomorrow night. The museum has a number of new works that have been lent to us by several discerning art collectors. I'd love for all of you to attend," Leonor told them again. "The food is being catered, of course, and promises to be excellent. Not as good as yours, Madeline, but almost," she qualified with a warm smile.

Madeline laughed, delighted. "We'll definitely come, won't we?" Her eyes swept over her son and daughter, coming to rest on her husband's face.

"Wouldn't miss it," RJ told his half sister. "I've got the invitations on my dresser bureau."

Just then they heard the front door opening and then closing again. A moment later, a tall, scowling, younger-looking version of RJ walked in.

"Barret, you missed lunch," RJ said with a reproving note in his voice. "Your aunt Leonor is here and—"

"I know who she is, Dad," Barret said sharply, cutting his father off. He nodded curtly at Leonor.

The annoyed look on RJ's face deepened. "I was about to introduce you to our guest, Joshua Pendergrass," he told Barret coldly. "He's—"

"Is he with 'Aunt' Leonor?" Barret asked, cutting off his father again.

RJ's eyes narrowed. He was obviously embarrassed by his oldest son's abruptness and at a loss as to how to get him to behave properly.

"Yes. He—"

"Then I don't need to know anything else." Turning toward his mother, Barret said, "I already ate, Mom." And with that, he left the room.

"I'm sorry you had to see that," RJ apologized to Leonor and his guest. "You'd think that once they were out of their teens, they'd learn how to behave like civilized human beings again. Unfortunately," he sighed, "that doesn't always happen."

"You'll have to forgive our oldest," Madeline said to Leonor and Josh. "He's been going through a rough patch, trying to find himself."

"Not exactly a challenge, Madeline," RJ said, clearly embarrassed as well as annoyed. "He's the tall kid with the miserable personality."

"I'm still sorry you had to see that," Madeline apologized, trying to smooth things over. "Barret's not usually like that."

"No, sometimes he's asleep," RJ interjected, obviously as upset, in his own way, as his wife was over his son's behavior. "I guess we'll just have to be happy that two of the kids turned out well," he concluded, looking at Braden and Celia.

"Well, Barret's welcome to come tomorrow night, too—as long as he promises not to throw rocks or anything else at the paintings," Leonor cautioned. She was only half kidding.

"Don't worry, if I can't get him to clean up his act, I won't give him his invitation," RJ promised.

"We might all have a better time if he doesn't go," Braden commented, finally adding in his two cents.

"Can we take a vote on that?" Celia asked, looking around the table.

"We'll see if he's in a better mood tomorrow," Madeline suggested. "He can be a really lovely person when he wants to be."

RJ murmured something under his breath, but didn't bother repeating it.

A few minutes later, he and Madeline walked his sister and guest to the front door. "Well, except for one hiccup, all in all I'd say it was a nice meal." RJ hugged Leonor as did his wife. "You really need to come around more often, Leonor."

"I will," she promised. "And we'll see you tomorrow."

She didn't notice the pensive look on Josh's face as they took their leave of her brother and his family.

Chapter 17

Josh tried to refrain from saying anything for as long as possible, but the more he thought about Barret Hartman's rude behavior toward Leonor, the more annoyed he felt himself becoming.

Finally, he couldn't keep quiet any longer. Sparing a glance toward Leonor as he drove her back to her house, Josh asked point-blank, "Exactly what is that kid's problem?"

Leonor shrugged, hoping that he wouldn't pursue the subject any further. "Oh, he's not so bad."

"He's not so good, either," Josh countered. "Seriously, what's his problem with you?" he wanted to know.

Leonor pressed her lips together. For a moment, she was unwilling to say anything. But then she sighed and answered Josh's question, at least to the best of her ability.

"You know how some people can never have enough money, no matter how much money they actually have?"

"Go on," he encouraged. He had a feeling he wasn't going to like what he was about to hear.

"Well, my nephew Barret kind of falls into that category."

That didn't answer anything, Josh thought. "What does that have to do with the kid's sullen attitude toward you?"

Considering the fact that Josh had delved into her family's dynamics in trying to assess Livia's hold over them, she wasn't sure just how much family history he already knew. "My father left half his money to RJ and half to me."

She'd already mentioned something to that effect, Josh recalled. "Seems fair."

"Let's just say, not to everyone," she told him, thinking of Barret, "especially considering that Livia stole Robert Hartman—my father—away from his first wife."

Josh thought back to the man sitting across from them at the table. Leonor's half brother seemed rather friendly, but Josh knew people could put on elaborate acts if it suited their purposes.

"Does RJ feel that way?" he wanted to know.

"I gather he did at one point," Leonor answered honestly. "He brought a suit against my mother—and me. But the judge ruled against him, and eventually, he came to terms with that."

"But Barret didn't?" Josh guessed.

She didn't feel comfortable about pointing fingers. Barret was, after all, family. Because of that, she cut the young man a lot of slack.

When she spoke, it was without blame. "Barret's an angry young man who needs something to be angry about. He'll get over it."

Her reaction seemed exceptionally mild to him, under the circumstances. Her nephew's eyes had been almost shooting daggers at her. "You seem awful laid-back about the whole thing."

Leonor laughed good-naturedly. "Well, I've had to suffer a great many slings and arrows because of who my mother was and is. In comparison, this is nothing. Trust me," she assured him.

Josh had his doubts about that. Shrugging, he allowed, "If you say so."

"I say so," she replied with a note of finality that surprised him. She was, in effect, telling him that the topic was off-limits.

Josh brought her to her house.

Parking his vehicle in the street, he got out and came around to the passenger side. As he was about to open that door, she informed him, "I'm perfectly capable of getting out of your car."

Josh pulled the door open. "No one said that you're not."

Closing the door again, he walked beside her as she approached her front door.

"Now what are you doing?" she asked him, watching him warily.

"Walking you to your door," he replied mildly.

"You don't have to do that," she informed him. "This wasn't a date," she insisted.

"Maybe it slipped your mind," he brought up, "but someone tried to run you over twice now, so yes, I do."

She frowned. He was getting a little carried away in her opinion. Maybe he had managed to scare off the threat and it was over. "You expect someone to run me over in front of my house?"

She began to walk and he came right along with her. It seemed to her that Josh was bound and determined to make sure no harm came to her. She supposed that did have a nice feeling to it.

"Bad guys have been known to be creative," he told her as he escorted her to her door.

"So have FBI agents," she pointed out flippantly.

She was offering resistance. He'd expected nothing less from her. "If I were that creative, I would have never told you who I was."

"Maybe that was all part of your plan to get me to trust you," she countered. Leonor put her key into the front door, then looked at him over her shoulder. She was wavering and weighing pros and cons of her next words. Finally, she said, "Well, since you're here, would you like to come in for a nightcap?"

She watched as just a hint of a sexy smile began

to cover his mouth. "Would it damage my trustworthiness if I said yes?"

"I'll have to think about that one." Even so, Leonor left her door open for him as she walked into her house.

Josh never lost a step following her in.

"Nice place," he commented, looking around. "It's actually a lot simpler looking than I expected," he confessed.

"I sent the throne out to be cleaned," Leonor deadpanned.

He nodded his head, never missing a beat. "That would explain it."

She made her way into the small kitchen and opened her refrigerator. "Beer or whiskey?" she offered.

"Beer. Whiskey's too potent," he explained, adding, "You're intoxicating enough as it is."

"Is that the best you've got?" she challenged. Taking out two bottles of beer, she handed Josh one.

He took it, but his attention was elsewhere. "I haven't even gotten warmed up yet," he told her.

Josh allowed himself one long sip of the dark brew. They sat down on her gray sofa. As he placed the bottle of beer on the coffee table, he glanced at her profile—and noticed something he hadn't before. It made him smile.

Catching his expression, she asked, "What?"

His eyes crinkled as he answered, "You've got freckles."

Her hand instantly went up to her cheek, covering the offending area. "No, I don't," she denied.

"Then how did you know where to put your hand to cover them?" he asked, amused by her reaction.

Leonor stiffened. She always tried to put makeup over her freckles. She'd always hated them. Freckles belonged on children, not on grown women.

"Did you come here to make me feel self-conscious?" she asked.

He drew her hand away from her cheek. "Freckles look good on you," he told her. "And no, I came here because I wanted to make sure you got in safe."

She blew out a breath. "Well, I'm in. Safe. You're free to go."

A self-mocking smile curved his mouth. "You'd think so, wouldn't you?"

"Why aren't you leaving?" she wanted to know, her voice dropping to a lower octave. The way he was looking at her was swiftly dissipating her resolve.

"Because," Josh confessed, his voice as low as hers, "you seem to have this power over me, making me want to take you into my arms and kiss you."

She could feel her heart starting to pound. Leonor raised her eyes to his. She barely had enough breath within her to ask, "So what's stopping you?"

"Damned if I know," he whispered.

The next second, Josh drew her into his arms, pulling her in very close. Close enough to feel his heart echoing hers.

And then he kissed her.

It didn't end there.

But they both knew that it wouldn't.

Unlike the first time, they knew exactly what to

expect, what was waiting for them, and they immersed themselves in each another with both familiarity and abandonment.

Clothes fell away without ceremony as vivid memories of the other night were revisited, re-created and, if possible, improved on.

Everything was strikingly familiar and yet at the same time, new and different from before.

It occurred to Leonor that between that first time and now, she had merely been sleepwalking, waiting to revisit the sheer ecstasy that she had experienced the first time she and Josh had made love together.

To her sheer delight, she discovered that she hadn't been mistaken. The passion, the desire, the thrill were every bit as wondrous this time as they had been the first time.

And one other thing.

She found that she wanted more. She wanted to experience it again and again.

There was no satisfaction at the end of the evening. Oh, there was in the strictest interpretation of the word, but it was the feeling of having reached something, achieved something. It wasn't an all-consuming satisfaction.

She knew at that moment that no matter how many times she and Josh made love, she would find herself yearning for the next time, even while she was being gratified at that very moment.

And that worried her.

Even as exhaustion took hold of her, claiming her very last vital breath and secretly dictating that she seek rejuvenation through sleep, Leonor realized that she would never stop wanting what was happening. Never stop wanting Josh.

And that, she knew, put her at a terrible disadvantage.

When she woke up the next morning, Leonor realized that she was alone in her bed.

Bolting upright, she was about to call out for him to see if he was still somewhere in the house.

His name died on her lips a second before she ever uttered it. Josh was in the corner of the bedroom, pulling on his pants.

Sensing she was awake, he looked at her over his shoulder and flashed a smile at her.

"Sorry," he apologized. "I didn't mean to wake you," Josh said. "I've got to get back to my hotel room and into my tux for that gala you're holding at the museum."

Leonor tucked the sheet around her as she remained sitting up. "You have a tuxedo?" she questioned, trying to picture him in one.

He wondered just how uncivilized she thought the agents in the Bureau were. "I told you, we're always prepared."

"Are you with the FBI or the Boy Scouts?" she asked, amused.

He laughed at the image that created in his mind. "A little bit of both, actually," he told her. Josh crossed back to her, pausing by the bed. "You going to be okay?"

His concern was touching, even though she told herself it could all still be an act.

"I'll be fine," she assured him.

Looking around for his shirt, he told her, "I'll come by and pick you up for this thing."

"I do know the way there," she reminded him. The last thing she wanted was a keeper—or to have him think of her as helpless.

He loved the way sleepiness still clung to her, loved the way her hair was mussed up, like a soft, red tornado. "Humor me."

The corners of her mouth curved. "I thought that was what I was doing last night."

"Oh, is that what you call it now?" he wanted to know. "Humoring me?"

Leonor turned her face up to his, already feeling her pulse ratcheting up even faster. "Why, what would you call it?"

Josh sat back down on the bed. "Sheer ecstasy," he told her, punctuating his statement with a light kiss on her lips—which turned out to be his mistake. Because he couldn't stop with just one kiss and he knew it.

A second kiss only necessitated more, and suddenly, he found himself shedding the clothes that he had just put on.

The next moment, he was crawling back into bed with her for just one more encore of last night.

It turned out to be a very long encore.

"I should be there by now," Leonor complained more than an hour later, hurrying into a particularly stunning silvery green cocktail dress that accentuated her small waist and clung to her supple hips with every step that she took.

"We saved time by showering together," Josh pointed out.

"That did *not* save time," she reminded him. It had been a first for her. The first time that she had ever made love in the shower.

Josh's grin was a bit crooked as he admitted, "No, I guess that it really didn't." He forced himself to think logically and stop picturing her nude and willing in his arms. "We just need to swing by my hotel room so I can get that tux. All I need is a couple of minutes to get into it," he told her.

She knew exactly where another state of undress might lead and she really couldn't afford for that to happen again.

"How about you meet me at the museum when you're done?" she suggested, keenly aware of the minutes that were ticking away.

"Just a couple of minutes," Josh repeated firmly.

"Nobody on earth can get dressed that fast," Leonor protested.

"I can," he informed her. "Life-and-death situations can train a guy to do all sorts of things."

She knew she was destined to lose this argument and they were wasting time by even having it.

"Okay," she agreed reluctantly. "But if you're *not* ready in a couple of minutes," she warned, "I'm calling a cab. Better yet, I'll confiscate your car and *you* call a cab," she told him.

"Careful," he told her, a dangerously sexy look entering his eyes, "feisty women really turn me on."

"I'm not saying another word," she promised, raising her right hand in a solemn vow as she used her other hand to help slip on her high heels.

Twenty minutes later, after first swinging by Josh's hotel room for what amounted to the fastest change of clothing she had ever witnessed, they pulled up in front of the art museum.

Leonor looked at her watch in disbelief as she got out of his vehicle.

A valet quickly stepped up to take the sedan and park it for them in the structure.

As if reading her mind, Josh said, "Told you we'd be here in record time."

"Arrogance is not a becoming trait," Leonor pretended to chide.

"I'll be sure to work on that," Josh promised.

His hand against the small of her back, he guided her into the building she knew like the back of her hand. He scanned the area. It had become an ingrained habit with him, like breathing.

"Looks like we're practically the first ones here," he observed.

"Go grab yourself some champagne and stand around looking impressive," she suggested. "That shouldn't be hard for you to do," Leonor added with an appreciative smile.

He never found himself at loose ends for something to do. Besides, she was his concern at the moment. "What about you?"

"I've got a thousand things to see to before this thing officially gets underway," she answered, already walking away.

Lengthening his stride, Josh fell into step right beside her.

"I'll help," he offered. "That way it'll go faster."

Leonor laughed. "You 'help' and I'll really fall behind." She gave it another try. "Do me a favor. Just stand around and look pretty," she told him. Then, knowing what he was thinking, Leonor told him, "Nothing is going to happen to me here. Before you know it, dozens of people will be milling around. And then hundreds. I'll be perfectly safe, right out here in plain sight."

Leonor patted his cheek, then rising up on her toes and leaning in, she whispered, "Relax, Special Agent Howard. Nothing's going to happen."

He wished he was as confident as she was. But his gut was telling him otherwise.

Guts, he'd been told by his superior, had no scientific data to back claims that they could reliably predict the way any particular thing would turn out. But there was no denying that he trusted his gut more than he trusted the word of a so-called informant or any statistical data he might be saddled with.

While he was well aware that he couldn't shadow Leonor's every step today at the gala, he was still determined to watch her as much as was humanly possible. He intended to keep an eye on Leonor whether she was dashing off to talk to the caterer, or pausing to momentarily smooth Sheffield's ruffled feathers. Or diplomatically reassuring one of the newest museum donors that his three Monets were as safe here as they were when they were hanging in his high-security monitored Swiss chalet.

Safer, perhaps, and definitely far more appreciated.

Though at times it was far from easy and a bit tricky, Josh managed to keep his eyes on Leonor at all times. Most of those times, he even found a way to join her, being at his most charming and mingling with the patrons, all of whom, he knew, Sheffield was hoping had brought their checkbooks and their generosity. The latter was being liberally plied with very expensive champagne and wines, all of which had been donated for tonight's cause by local patrons.

Josh smiled to himself as he once again shadowed Leonor's movements. Maybe he was in the wrong line of work. And then again, he amended, watching Leonor, maybe he was just where he was supposed to be.

Chapter 18

Josh wasn't sure just exactly how it happened. One moment he was standing right next to Leonor, struggling to keep his eyes from shutting as one of the museum's more active—and generous—patrons, Baxter Ward, was droning on and on about how he believed that Jackson Pollock's work didn't hold a candle to that of some of the earlier impressionists.

The man went on to heatedly rattle off names of artists that Josh had admittedly never heard of, talking about them as if they were beloved old friends.

The next moment, Leonor was unexpectedly excusing herself for a moment to "check on something in the back room." Josh thought it was code for escaping the droning patron and was about to volunteer to come with her, but Baxter grabbed his wrist.

For a rather small man, Baxter had an amazingly vise-like grip.

"Really," Baxter stressed with feeling, "Don't you agree that Pollock's just overrated?"

"Absolutely," Josh agreed, thinking that was the best way to disengage himself from the man's hold. It was obvious that he wasn't about to stop until he had won over a convert. "Now if you'll excuse me—"

However, Baxter didn't appear ready to release his captured audience, especially after having lost Leonor. Taking a breath, the man seemed like he was getting his second wind.

"Oh, but I haven't finished telling you about—" Baxter began to protest.

"Hold that thought," Josh said, finally managing to successfully wrench his wrist free from Baxter's grip. "I'll be right back."

In another life, Josh added silently, hurrying to catch up to Leonor. He'd seen her slip into the back hallway.

Since it wasn't to have a word with Sheffield—the director was right in the main room, holding court—he wasn't sure why Leonor had suddenly darted away but he wasn't about to risk having her wander off somewhere without him.

Yes, the museum was full of people but things were just as likely to go bad in a crowd as they were in a back alley.

Frustrated, Josh turned a corner. He wasn't about to have anything happen to Leonor just because she insisted on being so damn pigheaded and independent.

Turning a second corner, he saw her. Leonor was walking back toward the main room. Not about to wait for her to reach him, Josh hurried over to her.

"What do you think you're doing?" he demanded, lowering his voice so that only she heard. There was enough of a din coming from the main gallery to drown out their voices. "You're not supposed to run off like that, especially without telling me."

A fleeting, annoyed look creased her brow. "No matter what you think, you're not in charge of me, Josh. And I certainly don't need your 'permission' to go to the ladies' room."

"Oh." The ladies' room? That temporarily took the wind out of his sails. He struggled to regain ground. "Well, you should have told me anyway, I would have walked you."

She had to press her lips together to keep from laughing.

"This is *not* preschool. Nobody goes to the restroom in pairs." That was when she caught sight of two women walking into the facility she'd just vacated, talking animatedly about one of the paintings. She saw the smug expression on Josh's face. "All right, *almost* nobody," she amended.

"You're still not out of danger," he reminded her. She was an intelligent woman; she knew better. Why did he have to keep having this same argument with her? Didn't she want to stay safe?

"The only danger I'm in is being smothered to death," she informed him glibly. "Look, I know that you have good intentions, but—"

He saw the flash out of the corner of his eye and reacted instantly. Grabbing Leonor, he pushed her behind him. He shielded her with his own body at the same time that he pulled out his weapon.

Josh aimed and fired.

It had become second nature to him, as had hitting what he aimed for.

The assailant, a dark-haired man of medium height, dressed in a tuxedo which had allowed him to blend in with nearly half the population in the museum, dropped to the floor instantly.

Blood flowed from the single bullet now lodged in his throat. It pooled beneath his upper torso, discoloring the tan travertine floor. The shooter sputtered for less than half a minute, then stopped, his eyes glazing over. He was gone.

Still holding his weapon in case the shooter hadn't acted alone, Josh bent over the assailant and checked his pulse.

There was none.

Rising again, he turned toward Leonor, who was standing less than six inches behind him. She was looking very pale.

"Do you recognize this man?" he asked her.

She took in a small breath. "No, never saw him before in my—"

She didn't finish her sentence.

Turning even paler, Leonor's knees gave way. She would have sunk to the floor where she stood if he hadn't moved quickly and caught her. That was when he saw the bullet hole in the silver-green material in the vicinity of her chest.

There was blood oozing out of it.

Drawn by what sounded like firecrackers mixing with the din of sharply raised voices and sporadic laughter, several people had hurried into the rear hallway.

The sight of the lifeless shooter between them and the man with the gun had them stopping dead in their tracks.

"Call 9-1-1," Josh ordered.

Stunned, one of the women who had just come out of the ladies' room behind them looked as if she was going to pass out herself.

She stared at Leonor. "Is she—?" she stammered, unable to continue.

"Call 9-1-1!" Josh repeated, shouting the words this time.

Several people pulled out their cell phones, their voices talking over one another as they made calls to the police department.

Josh knew he should put Leonor down on the floor as gently as possible, that any movement at all might be ill-advised for her, but he just couldn't get himself to relinquish his hold, couldn't get himself to take his arms away from her body. It was as if something told him that if he broke this frail connection between them, she was going to die.

So he went on holding Leonor in his arms, unmindful of the blood soaking into his jacket and shirt.

Her blood.

"Open your eyes, Leonor," he ordered. When her eyes remained closed, the same words he'd just uttered became a plea. "Leonor, c'mon, baby, open your eyes. You can't just give up. You're a fighter, remember? You can't let whoever hired that thug to win, do you hear me?"

He was raising his voice now, competing with the sound of an approaching siren.

"It's almost here, baby. The ambulance is almost here. It's going to take you to the hospital and you're going to be all right, you hear me? You're going to be fine. I'm not going to let you die on me."

Leonor's eyelids fluttered and then opened, just for a split second.

"You…are…the…world's…bossiest…man," she managed to whisper before her eyelids shut again.

The sound of her voice gave him hope. "Say it again, Leonor," he begged, holding on to her tightly. "Say it again."

The paramedics arrived at that moment. Before either man could ask any questions, Josh volunteered the crucial information: "She sustained a single bullet to the chest. The shooter's dead. He needs a coroner, not an ambulance."

"Put her down gently," the head paramedic instructed, steadying the gurney. Josh did as he was told. "Okay, step back," the man told him.

He and his partner secured Leonor onto the gurney, then immediately hurried back out to the ambulance.

"What's going on?" Sheffield demanded indignantly, then practically swallowed his tongue when he realized what was happening. "Is she—?"

"No!" Josh all but shouted, quickening his pace to keep up with the gurney.

"Steady," the first paramedic warned his partner as they retracted the gurney's legs and loaded it onto the ambulance.

Once they had Leonor inside, Josh began to climb in, as well.

"Sorry, buddy, but you're going to have to follow us in your car," the paramedic in charge told him.

"The hell I will," Josh snapped. He pulled out his FBI badge and ID. "I'm coming with you."

Spying Josh's weapon, the paramedic backed off. "Fine, no argument. But we'd better hurry before she bleeds out," the man told him.

"Then start driving!" Josh bit off.

The second paramedic scrambled into the driver's seat.

Josh held her hand all the way to the hospital, willing his life force into her.

Josh didn't remember the trip, hardly remembered getting off the ambulance, and then running beside it as the paramedics guided the gurney in through the electronic ER doors.

Vital statistics were rattled off as the paramedics turned their patient over to the ER crew.

Josh felt helpless and in the way, but refused to step aside. He accompanied Leonor all the way to exam room one, at which time the room's swinging doors closed, barring his access.

Frustrated, Josh stood guard right outside the doors, watching through the small windows as an ER team worked over her. He desperately wanted to be in there with her, holding her hand, bullying her into clinging to life, but he knew he'd only be in the way. He knew that right now, the important thing was to stabilize her and stop the bleeding.

Josh stood there, keeping vigil, for more than an hour. When the doors finally opened again, instead of the ER doctor coming out to give him an update on how everything had gone, Josh saw two nurses and an orderly guiding Leonor's gurney toward the elevator. A doctor joined them.

His heart began to pound wildly as a sense of dread filled him. He followed behind the team. "What's going on?" he demanded.

"She has a lot of internal bleeding," one of the nurses told him. "We need to operate."

He couldn't remember the last time he had felt sheer panic.

He felt it now.

"But she's going to make it, right? Right?" he demanded.

"She's young, she's strong and her chances look favorable, but I'm not God—" the doctor accompanying the gurney told him.

Josh caught hold of the surgeon's arm for just a moment, his eyes pinning the doctor's. "Today you better hope you are," he ordered. Regaining control, he released the surgeon's arm.

One of the nurses took pity on him. "There's a

waiting room for family and friends right next to the operating room. You can wait for word there."

Josh gave her a grateful look and got on just before the doors closed.

He'd never known time to move so slowly.

It felt as if every second had been dipped in molasses before it attempted to drag itself toward the next second.

Josh occupied himself by pacing the length of the empty waiting room. He thought about calling several of Leonor's siblings, but he didn't know any of their phone numbers and he couldn't seem to pull his head together sufficiently enough to attempt to locate them.

Even if he had those phone numbers, what would he say to her brothers and sisters? "Leonor's been shot and might very well be clinging to life, so get yourself down here ASAP?"

And then do what, he silently demanded. Pace around like helpless jackasses?

Like me?

There was only room for one jackass in the waiting room, he thought irritably, blowing out a deep, ragged breath.

It was better if he notified them *after* Leonor recovered.

And she *was* going to recover, he thought fiercely. He wasn't about to let her do anything else. That wasn't negotiable.

As if it's up to you, he mocked himself.

Fury spiked through his veins. He couldn't even

manage to keep her safe, so how was he supposed to bully God into making her recover?

Damn, he'd never felt so helpless before in his life, he thought, pacing around the waiting room's perimeter again.

He had no idea how long he walked.

Josh stopped looking at his watch. After that he completely lost track of time.

It felt as if he had put in at least ten miles pacing and he was exhausted. But he just couldn't get himself to sit down. He knew if he did sit down, he was liable never to get up again.

Three and a half hours after Leonor had been wheeled into the third floor operating room someone finally came into the waiting room and called out Josh's name.

Facing away from the doorway, Josh practically spun around on his heel to face the person who had said his name.

"I'm Joshua Howard," he said, cutting across the room in the blink of an eye. "How is she?" The look on his face dared the doctor to tell him anything other than she was all right.

"It was touch and go for a while," the cardiothoracic surgeon, Dr. Steven Mayer, told him with a grim expression. "But we stopped the bleeding and she looks pretty good."

"She's going to recover?" Josh pressed, needing to hear those words.

The surgeon nodded. "She's going to recover. She's going to hurt for a few weeks, but she most definitely will recover." His grim expression gave way to a meager smile. "She's a fighter, that one."

"Yeah, I know," Josh said, the words all but whooshing out of him. He had never experienced such an overwhelming sense of relief in his life. Grabbing the doctor's hand, he shook it, hard. "Thank you!" he said, his voice cracking in the middle of the word.

"My pleasure," Mayer replied with sincerity.

Dropping his hand to his side, Josh looked over the surgeon's shoulder toward the operating room doors. "Can I see her?"

"She's in recovery right now. They'll move her to her room in about an hour or so. A nurse will take you to her there and you can be with Ms. Colton. Until then, I suggest that you get yourself something to eat." The small, deep-set brown eyes swept over Josh. "And I'd also take off that jacket and maybe see about getting it to the cleaners. There's a lot of blood on it," Mayer pointed out. "I hear they work miracles these days."

Josh looked down at his jacket for the first time since Leonor had been shot. It looked like hell. No wonder people had been giving him strange looks.

But the tuxedo jacket was the least of his concerns right now, although Mavis, the woman at the Bureau who ran the wardrobe area they were sometimes forced to turn to, was undoubtedly going to have a choice word or two to offer him when he brought the tuxedo back to her.

He'd pay for another one, he thought.

Stripping off the jacket, Josh turned it inside out,

hiding the blood. He tossed it on the arm of the closest chair.

"I'll take care of it later," he murmured.

"Cafeteria's in the basement," Mayer told him as he began to walk away. "Vending machines are located in the middle hallway, just past the elevators."

And with that, he was gone.

Josh toyed with the idea of the cafeteria and quickly discarded it. He wasn't hungry. His stomach had closed up shop the instant that he'd realized Leonor had been shot. Thinking back, he vaguely recalled having a couple of things off the buffet tables at the museum, but that hadn't been because he was hungry; it was more like a sense of boredom had propelled him to have something to do with his hands. Eating seemed like the logical choice at the time.

Now the thought of food had his stomach threatening to mutiny.

So he continued pacing, waiting for the nurse to come tell him that Leonor was being moved from recovery to her room.

Once he knew that Leonor was there and safe, he had a few things to tend to. But he didn't like the idea of leaving her alone like that, not after what had just happened. He didn't think there would be another attempt made on her life tonight, but he was taking no chances. Besides, he needed to have a few questions answered first. Questions like who the shooter had been and who had hired him to kill Leonor. Since she hadn't recognized him, he was fairly certain that the shooter was a hit man. Until he knew who had hired the assassin, he wasn't going to feel that Leonor was safe.

Maybe he *should* call Mac, he decided. He'd fill the man in on what had happened and ask him to stick around Leonor's room until he got back. She'd definitely be safe with Mac watching over her.

Still too agitated to think clearly, Josh called the FBI tech back at the field office and asked Bailey to get Mac's phone number for him.

Chapter 19

For the next two days, Leonor drifted in and out of consciousness, mostly out. She was aware of people coming in and out of her room, moving like formless shadows in the background. There were people touching her, changing her dressings, taking out and putting in IVs. Voices droned on in her subconscious, saying things she couldn't grasp.

She was aware of other people coming into her room, people whose voices sounded concerned. They blended with her dreams and faded away, as well.

There were times she thought she heard Josh talking to her, saying things she couldn't really hear or understand, but she knew it was him. Knew because of the cadence of his voice.

Words would drift in and out of her head, leaving only the faintest impression, if they left any at all.

The one thing she was aware of was that every time she tried to open her eyes—only vaguely aware that she succeeded once in a while—there was always the feeling that there was someone in her room.

Trying to open her eyes was exhausting. Most of the time, she'd slip mercifully back into an inky darkness, a place where the radiating pain she'd felt exploding into her chest couldn't find her.

This went on, Leonor was later able to piece together, for close to three days before she finally managed to anchor her brain to reality and began to take tentative steps toward pulling the world into perspective and to recover.

The tall, slender, solemn-looking blonde in the nurse's uniform silently slipped into the hospital room, easing the door closed behind her.

She knew every inch of the hospital, so coming in undetected had been easy for her.

Her back against the door, the older woman carefully studied the pale face of the patient lying so still in the bed that was a few feet away from her.

She watched the eyes, waiting to see if they would open.

They remained closed.

After several beats had gone by, the woman ventured forward. Making her way to the window, she very quietly lowered the blinds until the room was submerged in darkness.

Again she looked at the patient's eyes.

Satisfied that the other remained unconscious, the woman retraced her steps and paused by the bed. Giving in to a momentarily surge of sentiment, the woman in the nurse's uniform moved the tray with its single glass of water out of the way. She wanted to get closer.

Leonor had sensed more than heard the door to her room opening and then softly closing again. And she *felt* rather than saw someone—a nurse?—draw close to her bed.

The light, familiar scent wove seductively around her, stirring her memory.

Reminding her.

Like so many times these last few days, Leonor struggled fiercely to open her eyes, to make some sort of noise to let the person in the room know that she knew she was there. But she couldn't. Both tasks were completely out of the realm of her capabilities, at least for now.

But still she tried and she must have succeeded to some small degree because the person with her murmured, "Go on sleeping, kiddo. You need your strength."

Kiddo.

Her mother used to call her that. Her mother wore that perfume.

Was she here? In the hospital room? Was Livia *here* with her?

Again Leonor struggled to lift her eyelids but

it was as if they were glued shut with five-pound weights holding each in place.

Her eyelids refused to budge, no matter how hard she tried to pry them open.

And then, just for a fleeting second, she could have sworn she felt warm breath on the side of her face. On her cheek.

The next moment, that same voice whispered, "You won't have to worry about him anymore, kiddo. I took care of him. He won't be sending anyone else to try to kill you." A low, guttural sound—a laugh?—separated the sentences. "You were the only one who was ever worth a damn."

Livia.

It had to be Livia.

Why couldn't she open her eyes? Why couldn't she just wake up when she wanted to?

Exhausted, Leonor went on struggling, went on trying to open her eyes. Trying to surface from the deep, murky darkness that had such a hold on her.

And then, finally, after what seemed like forever, Leonor managed to open her eyelids.

Clutching the raised bed railings on either side of her, Leonor dragged herself up into a semisitting position, grunting in pain as she did so.

"Mother?"

Josh had been in her room for the last twenty minutes, getting back to her as soon as he had verified for himself what Arroyo had called to tell him.

Finding her asleep as always, he had gone to stand

by the window. He was looking out now, wondering if Leonor was ever going to regain consciousness for more than a few seconds at a time.

When he heard her voice, he instantly swung around and crossed to her bed, half-afraid that he was imagining things again. It wouldn't be the first time that he thought he heard her voice.

But this time, he actually had.

Thrilled, he could hardly believe it. "You're awake!"

He wanted to hug her, but was afraid to at the same time. Leonor looked so fragile he was leery of hurting her.

Leonor was looking around wildly. "Where is she?" she cried.

He took hold of her shoulders, gently pushing her back down onto the bed. "Where's who?"

She struggled to sit up again, frustrated. "Mother." Her eyes were wide as she turned them to Josh. "She was right here, in this room," Leonor insisted, "talking to me."

"Honey." Having succeeded in getting her to lie down again, he took her hand in his. Everything about her felt as if it could just break up into tiny pieces at the least bit of pressure. "You're just imagining things."

"No, she was here," Leonor insisted. "She was wearing a nurse's uniform, but it was her. She was wearing that perfume she always wears."

Josh still believed that Leonor was imagining things. "You've been through a lot, Leonor. Your brain is playing tricks on you, combining bits and pieces from your memory," he said soothingly.

"No, she was here. I know it," Leonor cried adamantly. "She called me 'kiddo.' Nobody ever calls me that. I never liked it, but she called me that anyway."

He'd insisted on having a guard posted right outside Leonor's room around the clock. Could Livia have slipped in anyway? He was inclined to say no, but he'd learned that the woman was incredibly resourceful, so the possibility did exist.

Still, he tried to tell Leonor that it was only her imagination at work.

"Just some of the things that your brain was combining," he told her gently, taking a seat next to her bed.

"No," Leonor maintained, "she was here. I heard her moving things. Her prints have to be on *something.*" And then the blinds caught her eye. "Are the blinds usually closed like that?"

He looked at the far side now. That side faced a tall office building across the street. "No, as a matter of fact, they're usually open."

"Livia must have closed the blinds," Leonor concluded excitedly. "And she said something to me." Her head was hurting, and it was hard pulling her thoughts together, hard remembering. "She said...she said she 'took care of him.' That 'he' wouldn't be paying anyone to hurt me again." Almost exhausted, Leonor appealed to the man who had saved her life—in more ways than one. "She was here, I *know* Livia was here."

Stunned, Josh could only look at her. He had just

gotten back from the medical examiner's office, back from viewing Leonor's nephew, Barret, laid out on a slab, an apparent suicide. RJ's oldest son had left a note confessing that he had been the one who had tried to have Leonor killed because he hated her, hated that she was connected to his family in any way and hated her for having stolen the money he felt rightfully belonged to his father because she'd had, according to the suicide note he'd left, "the audacity to be born."

"Did you *see* her close the blinds?" Josh asked. If Livia had closed them, then with any luck, she'd left her prints on them somewhere.

"No, but I know she had to." She looked at Josh. "Then you do believe me?"

"Anything's possible," Josh allowed. "I believe that *you* believe you and from everything I've learned about Livia Colton, she could have very possibly disguised herself as a nurse and slipped by the guard I've got posted outside your door." He just hoped that they wouldn't find a dead nurse somewhere on the premises, missing her uniform.

Taking out his cell phone, he called the field office's forensic team, telling them that he needed a hospital room dusted for prints—ASAP. He was rewarded with a deep, exaggerated sigh from the forensic team's leader, then the resigned promise that the team would be there as soon as possible.

Putting away his phone, Josh looked at the woman he had come so close to losing. He could see that Leonor was agitated, but at the same time, she was obviously struggling to keep her eyes open. Fatigue was winning out.

"Why don't you just get some sleep?" he suggested gently.

But Leonor was adamant. "No, I don't want to go to sleep. I don't know what I'll dream about if I fall asleep. I don't want to dream about Livia again," she said with feeling.

"For what it's worth," Josh told her, taking her hand in his again, "I don't think that was a dream."

Her face lit up. "Then you do believe me?"

"The Bureau's forensics team is coming to check it out, but yes, I believe you," he told her. "You couldn't have imagined that last part you told me she said to you. My guess is that wherever she was hiding out, Livia undoubtedly heard about what happened at the art museum—it's been all over the news for the last three days—and put two and two together. She came here to tell you that she took care of the problem and to reassure you that you can feel safe again."

Her brain just wasn't processing this. She thought of what Livia had said to her.

"What does that mean?" Leonor asked. "That she took care of 'him'? Took care of who?"

Josh thought of putting it off, of telling her about Barret and what he'd learned when she was stronger and up to hearing it.

But the news broadcasts were full of this latest development in the ongoing Colton saga—it seemed like people just couldn't get enough of this sensationalism—and he didn't want Leonor hearing it from some slicked-down, overpaid, plastic news anchor.

He knew he had to be the one to tell her.

"Well, they were ruling it a suicide, but with this new piece of information, I'd say it looks like Livia killed Barret Hartman."

"She *killed* him?" Leonor cried, shocked. "Why? Why would Livia kill RJ's son?"

"Because Barret was trying to kill you." Since he'd started this, he wanted Leonor to have all the facts. "Actually, Barret hired someone to kill you—three times," he added. "Apparently he wasn't any better at hiring a hit man than he was at 'finding himself.'" Josh recalled the words Barret's mother had used at lunch the other day when she was making excuses for his rude behavior.

Leonor's eyes filled with tears as she thought of the grief that her older brother and his family had to be going through right at this moment. None of this was making any sense to her.

"But why would Barret want to hurt me?" she wanted to know.

"Not hurt, *kill*," Josh corrected. "And it all boils down to jealousy and resentment. You had half the money he felt belonged to his father and ultimately, to him. In focusing on trying to get you killed, he didn't have to face up to the fact that he was an exceedingly poor excuse for a human being, a waste of skin who had never managed to accomplish a single worthwhile thing. And now, apparently, it turns out that he couldn't even hire a capable hit man. Something that I am very happy about."

Unable to help himself, he kissed the top of Leonor's head, gratitude flooding his heart.

Afraid that he would be tempted to *really* kiss her, Josh sat back in his chair.

"Did Livia say anything else while she was here?" he asked.

Leonor struggled to think for a moment, but coherence was getting progressively more difficult for her. Finally, a snatch of something came to her.

"I think I heard her say something to the effect that I was the only one who was ever worth a damn."

Josh laughed softly in response. "That does sound like her."

Leonor ran the tip of her tongue along her lips. They felt incredibly dry and it was getting harder and harder for her to talk. But she needed to tell him this. "Could you leave that out?"

He thought that was rather an odd request. He would have thought that the minute display of sentiment would have made her proud.

"What?"

Exhaustion was descending over her. She struggled to keep out of its grip just a little longer. "If you're writing a report, could you leave that part out?" she repeated.

It didn't seem to have any hidden meaning or deep significance to anything that was going on, so he had no problem going along with her wishes.

"All right, if that's what you want. But why?" he wanted to know.

"I don't want one of my brothers or sisters to accidentally come across that, you know, if that somehow got leaked to the press." She struggled, looking for words to make him understand. "I mean, we all suspected that Livia had no feelings for any of us, that she didn't love us or care about us—"

"Apparently she did about you," he interjected. Why else would the woman come out of hiding to eliminate Barret? No matter how invincible she thought she was, she did run the risk of getting caught.

Leonor shook her head, or at least thought she did. "I don't want that distinction. I don't want that to set me apart from the others. And most of all, I don't want my brothers and sisters thinking that Livia actually *could* love, but she chose not to love them."

"But to love you." Josh said what he knew was on her mind.

This time she did manage to shake her head. The room seemed to spin for a moment before settling down. "That's not love. What she did, she did because what Barret did offended her sense of self, that someone had the audacity to try to have one of her offspring eliminated."

Things began coming back to her, colliding in her brain as she tried to put them in order.

"There were rumors of Livia being seen in Vegas when Knox's son, Cody, was kidnapped. Cody turned up, safe and sound, and his kidnapper was found dead. That was probably her handiwork, too. She's got a thing about maintaining the Colton name."

Leonor shrugged, or tried to. Too late, she remembered her wound. Sharp, razor-edged pains sliced through her upper torso, making her wince.

She caught her lip between her teeth, trying to keep from crying out in pain.

"Let me call for the nurse, ask her to give you a sedative." Josh reached for the call button.

"No," Leonor begged. She tried to reach his arm, to stop him, but her fingers just brushed against the air, falling short. "Don't call her." The words came out in short, measured, urgent gasps. "Please. I don't want to get a sedative. All I need is you staying here with me, talking to me."

"Is that your polite way of saying I put you to sleep?" Josh asked with a laugh.

"No." She breathed heavily. "That's my way of saying that you make me feel like I'm safe. And if I feel safe, then maybe I can fall asleep—if you stay here long enough."

Josh wasn't convinced. He hated seeing her in pain. "I still think that a sedative would be the better way to go." As he said that, the forensics team he'd called entered the room. "Especially with these guys poking around, making noise."

"Hey, you asked us here, remember?" Roy Conway reminded Josh. He set his case down out of the way.

"I know."

As quickly as possible, Josh explained why he had

called them in. He needed to prove that Livia Colton had been here within the last few hours.

"You think she's still in the hospital somewhere?" Conway asked dubiously.

Josh sincerely doubted it. Livia Colton was too smart for that. "No, but at least it's a start in tracking her down."

"Famous last words," Conway said sarcastically. "If that woman doesn't want to be found, she's not going to be found. This isn't your average, run-of-the-mill simple-minded crook we're talking about. Don't forget," Conway said, lowering his voice as if to keep Leonor from hearing. "This lady built an empire."

Josh glanced over toward Leonor and saw that she had finally fallen back to sleep. "Funny thing about empires. They all wound up crumbling, no matter who they belonged to."

"Maybe you're right," Conway said. "All right, people, let's get to work."

With that, the forensic team began dusting for prints.

Chapter 20

"Try the blinds," Josh urged. When the head of the forensic team looked at him quizzically, Josh explained. "Leonor said that her mother might have pulled the blinds down. Maybe she wasn't careful and left behind at least a partial."

Nodding, Conway personally dusted the blinds for prints.

"Got a partial," the crime scene investigator announced several minutes later. Not wanting to get ahead of himself, he tempered his words. "It could belong to anyone."

"Then again, it could belong to Livia Colton," Josh countered.

Conway offered a ghost of a smile as he nodded. "There is that."

Taking the partial, Conway ran the print right then and there on his portable scanner. Livia's fingerprints had been in the system for over ten years, so finding a match, if there was one to be found, would not be a difficult matter.

"And we have a winner," Conway declared. Raising his eyes from the device he had used to match the partial, he looked up at Josh. "I gotta say, somebody up there must love you."

"I just live right," Josh quipped, then grew serious as he asked for a formal confirmation. "Then Livia Colton was here?"

Conway put the device carefully away. "Unless someone made off with her thumb, yeah, Livia Colton was here. Hell of a nervy woman," he commented.

"No argument," Josh agreed. "Pull everything you can from the surveillance cameras located on this floor and the first floor for the last five hours. Put all your people in the lab to work to see if they can find anyone who looks like Livia Colton entering this room. My guess is that Colton was probably dressed as a nurse. The guard outside Leonor's room said a nurse went in with medication on a tray. He didn't think anything of it at the time. Maybe it was her."

"You got it," Conway told him.

The forensic leader left with his team. There were enough samples packed in their cases to keep them busy for at least the next few days.

* * *

She woke up to find Josh sitting in the chair beside her bed. Slightly rumpled in appearance, he looked as if he'd been there all night.

Leonor took a deep breath, waiting to see if he would disappear, or if she actually saw him. Josh remained in the chair.

"You're still here."

The instant he heard her voice, he sat up and focused entirely on her.

And then he smiled. "Looks that way." He could feel his stiff, aching body protesting as he shifted in the chair.

That he was still here surprised her. After all, he had to know that she was on her way to recovery. "Don't you have a job to go to?"

He lightly ran his hand over her hair. She was conscious and there was a little bit of color in her face. When he thought of what *could* have been the outcome the other night, his blood ran cold.

"Right now," he told her, "watching over you *is* my job. By the way, some of the members of your family have been here, but you slept through that. I'll have the nurse call them, tell them you're conscious now."

But Leonor was still focused on the first part of his answer. "You're wasting your time if you think Livia's going to come back here. She's not," Leonor told him. She knew how her mother operated. The woman was devoid of maternal sentiments. "She delivered her message and now she's moved on."

"I know that."

Careful examination of the surveillance tapes had shown a woman matching Livia's description leaving the hospital via the rear loading dock fifteen minutes after she had been seen entering Leonor's room disguised as a nurse. There was no evidence that the woman ever came back.

Leonor didn't understand. "Then why are you still here?"

"Because you're still here," he told her simply. As a rule, Josh had never been an emotional man. But then, he had never been in love before and being in love, he'd found, had changed all the rules. "You almost died the other evening. I don't want to take a chance of that happening again."

Her brain still felt somewhat fuzzy. Had she missed something, she wondered. "Didn't you kill the hit man at the museum the other night?"

"Yes, I did." He was only sorry that he hadn't been able to get the man alive—and make him suffer for everything he had done to Leonor.

"And the man behind all that—" Her voice quavered for a moment before she forced herself to go on. "Barret," she finally managed to get out, "was—" Leonor paused for a moment before finally finding a word she could utter. "Eliminated."

Josh's eyes never left hers. Shouldn't she be getting more rest? Talking about this couldn't be any good for her. "He was."

She drew in a shaky breath and continued. "So if the threat had been neutralized and you're not waiting for Livia to pop up again, I don't understand. Why are you still here?" she wanted to know. "Shouldn't you be following up a new lead, tailing after someone else who can lead you to Livia?"

That would be the logical assumption, except for one thing. "I asked Arroyo to give the assignment to another special agent." He spoke carefully, his eyes never leaving her face. "And then I asked him for a leave of absence."

"Arroyo?" she questioned. Should she know that name? She was drawing a blank, Leonor thought.

He flashed her a smile, realizing that he might not have mentioned the man's name before. "He's the assistant director at the Bureau and my immediate supervisor."

"Oh." She thought for a moment, trying to organize the information he'd just given her. "I bet he wasn't happy."

Josh laughed drily. "That's putting it very diplomatically."

She realized the kind of repercussions Josh's request had to have had. "Aren't you afraid of what this could do to your career?"

He took her hand in his. She felt so frail he couldn't help thinking. "I don't care about my career. What I care about most is right here in this room." Since he'd admitted that, Josh decided to go for broke. "I know that because I lied to you about who I was, it's going to take you a long time to trust me again, but I was hoping that if I stuck around long enough, you might see your way to—"

"You don't know as much as you think you do," Leonor interjected, cutting him short.

She was putting him in his place, wasn't she? "I refuse to think that it's hopeless—"

"That's not what I said," she pointed out. She spoke slowly, trying not to run out of energy until they understood each another. "What I said is that you don't know as much as you think you do."

She saw the puzzled look on his face and did her best to explain. "Yes, you lied to me, but then, when I questioned you, you told me the truth and that took courage. I might have been angry that you misrepresented yourself but at bottom, I can understand why you did what you did. You had a job to do. You wanted to capture a dangerous fugitive." There was no other phrase she could use to describe the woman who had given her life and a great deal of baggage. "And you had to follow up any lead you thought you might have. I can't fault you for trying to do your job."

In view of everything, he felt that was exceedingly generous of Leonor. Another woman might have held his actions against him and told him to get lost.

"Then you think that you could eventually bring yourself to trust me?" he asked, mentally crossing his fingers.

"With my life," she told him honestly with a warm laugh.

The corners of Josh's mouth curved. "Your life, huh?"

Her eyes were smiling as she softly confirmed, "My life."

Her reply made him feel almost giddy. She forgave

him. He could feel a great weight being lifted off his shoulders. "Well, I know exactly where I want you to spend that life."

"Oh?" she asked, then gamely wanted to know, "And where's that?"

"With me."

There went her pulse again, she thought, feeling it accelerating. "Exactly what are you proposing?"

He took her hand in his again. "That's exactly it. I'm proposing."

Leonor could feel her jaw slacken and practically drop open, "To whom?" she asked cautiously, afraid of letting her thoughts run away with her.

"To you." His hands locked over hers, he drew them against his chest. "Leonor Colton, will you marry me?"

She was hearing the words, but somehow, they weren't penetrating. "You're serious?"

"Never more so in my whole life," he told her solemnly.

Stunned, Leonor could only stare at him for a long moment, speechless. When she finally did find her tongue, she tried to talk.

"I—" She got no further because Josh wouldn't let her.

Afraid she would turn him down, Josh talked quickly. "You don't have to give me an answer right now. I just want you to promise that you'll think about it. And while you're thinking about it, think about a couple of other things, too."

Josh had managed to arouse her curiosity. "Such as?" she asked.

"Such as, while you were in a coma, I had my old partner track down that no-good lowlife who stole your money and caused you so much grief with your family by splashing intimate details of their lives all over the internet, thanks to his insatiable avarice and desire for personal gain."

Leonor stared at him, dumbfound. "You found David?" she cried in disbelief. Why would he do that? "I never want to see that man again!" She began to cough. Raising her voice had irritated her throat.

He poured her a glass of water from the pitcher she had by her bed, then offered it to her.

She took the glass in both hands and drank, before giving it back to him.

"I don't blame you," he told her, setting the glass down next to the pitcher. "Don't worry. You won't have to see him. But you might want to know that he's under arrest and on his way to prison for stealing your money," he told her with a satisfied smile. "The good news is, the scum still had most of your money."

That was a surprise. She'd expected David to go through it, spending it on expensive toys that fed his ego.

"You recovered my money?" she asked in disbelief.

Josh nodded. "Consider it a bonus for what I put you through."

She didn't want him feeling guilty. "Josh, really, I don't—"

"I'm not finished," he told her, interrupting. "I still have something else to tell you."

She had no idea where this was going. Amusement curved the corners of her mouth. "Go ahead."

"I've decided that if you say yes to my proposal," he told her, closely watching her reaction to what he was about to say, "I'm going to resign from the Bureau."

She didn't want him doing that. "But you love being an FBI special agent," she protested.

"No," Josh corrected. "What I love is doing a good job, catching the bad guy, protecting people. There are other ways of doing that outside of the Bureau," he told her.

He could see she was about to protest again and he placed a finger against her lips, keeping her quiet until he could finish telling Leonor why he'd made this decision.

"If I remain with the Bureau, they more or less own me." It was just the way things were and until now, it hadn't mattered to him. But now it did. "They own my time whether or not I'm on the clock. I was thinking of starting up my own security firm," he told her. "That way, I'm my own boss, master of my own destiny." He saw her smiling. "What?"

Master of his own destiny, she thought, amused. "Sounds like you don't know the first thing about being married."

"Oh, I don't know about that," he countered. "I know that the first thing is to find someone you love more than anything in the world, and hell, I've already got that covered."

"Wait, back up," she instructed, his words replaying themselves belatedly in her head. "Say that again."

"I've already got that covered?" he said, asking if that was what she meant.

"No, the other part."

"That I know the first thing?" Josh asked her innocently.

Now she *knew* that he was toying with her. "The part between that and the other part."

It was hard keeping a straight face, but Josh managed it somehow. "Oh, you mean the part where I said that I've already found someone I love more than anything in the world?"

Finally! "Yes," she told him with a wide smile. "That part."

"I found someone I love more than anything in the world," he repeated obligingly.

There went her heart again, she thought, feeling it starting to pound. "You do?"

"I did, I have and I do." He paused as if to review the words he'd just said. "I think that covers everything," he told her.

Leonor looked up at him, her eyes saying things that she hadn't told him out loud yet. "Not yet," she prompted, waiting for him to "seal" the deal.

"Oh, how could I forget?" he murmured.

Lowering the guard railing on the side closest to him, Josh sat on the very edge of the hospital bed and gingerly gathered her into his arms, bringing her just close enough to him to kiss her.

He couldn't kiss her with the ardor he was feeling—she was still attached to a myriad of monitors and IVs—but he felt he still managed to sufficiently convey just what was waiting for her once she recovered.

Releasing Leonor—he was afraid that if he didn't, he might just give in to the demands created by the rush of desire surging through his veins—he murmured, "Anything else?"

Suspended just on the brink of the wondrous passions she'd already shared with him in her bed before all this had happened, Leonor took in a deep breath. "One more thing," she told him.

"What?"

"Yes," she breathed.

"Yes?" he repeated, not sure exactly what she was telling him.

"Yes," Leonor repeated again.

"Okay," he said, drawing out the word slowly as he watched her face for a further clue.

It was obvious that he wasn't following her, Leonor thought. He was trying so hard not to be pushy, he'd lost the thread. She found it for him by spelling out her meaning.

"Yes I will marry you."

A heady feeling of sheer joy swept over him. "You're sure?"

Her smile spread, encompassing him. "Very, very sure."

He pushed it a little further, just to be certain. "Even though I lied to you?"

She laughed. "Are you trying to talk me out of marrying you?"

"No, no, of course not," he said quickly.

"Then shut up and kiss me again," she ordered, humor shining in her eyes. "And this time kiss me like I'm your future wife, not a Vestal Virgin."

She knew that he wanted to, he thought, but he was trying to be cautious for her sake.

"I don't want to risk one of those IVs coming loose," he pointed out.

"We're in a hospital, Josh. If one of them comes loose, somebody will come to reattach me. That's what they're supposed to do. Now kiss me, Special Agent Howard, and remind me why I just said yes." Her smile turned sexy. "Think of it as upholding the honor of the Bureau."

"Yes, ma'am."

Josh took her into his arms again and kissed her with all the love that was brimming in his heart.

The honor of the Bureau was upheld just fine.

Epilogue

"You haven't changed your mind?" Leonor asked hesitantly.

Her question was directed to Josh. More than a week had passed since she'd been shot by the hit man her nephew had hired to kill her. More than a week since she had been inside her own home.

It felt almost strange now, crossing the threshold, entering her living room after having been in the hospital for all that time.

Forgoing the wheelchair that Josh had rented to help her get around, she'd declared that she wanted to walk into her house on her own two feet. They wound up compromising by leaving the wheelchair in his trunk, but he insisted that she at least allow him to hold on to her arm and help her into the house.

Her question, coming right after he'd closed the door behind them, caught Josh off guard.

"Changed my mind about what?" he asked as he guided her toward the sofa.

He wanted to take her straight to bed, but he knew Leonor would balk at that since she'd spent so much time in bed during her convalescence.

Leonor slowly sank down onto the sofa. The cushion felt welcoming beneath her. "About leaving the FBI and starting up your own security firm."

"I already put in my papers," he told her with a casual air.

Josh sat down next to her, thinking how good it was to have her back in this setting. How good it felt to have her *anywhere* after coming so close to losing her because of a stone-cold killer and the sociopath who had hired him.

"And they're okay with that?" she questioned. He was a good agent; would they just let him go like that?

"Well, they tried to talk me out of it by offering me a promotion, but I turned them down, saying that my mind was made up."

She didn't want him looking at her in a year or two and regretting what he'd impulsively done just because he thought that she'd wanted him to give up everything for her.

"Are you sure you're not going to be sorry you did this?" she pressed.

"Not a chance," he told her. "I know the way the Bureau works. They move their agents around the country like chess pieces, sending them where they'll be most effective at the time. You have a life in Austin and you want to stay close to your family. And I want to stay with you, so if my choice is between you and the Bureau, the choice is simple. I choose you." He brushed his lips against her temple and made her a promise. "You won't be sorry."

She grinned, "Not a chance. Unless, of course, you just keep kissing my temple."

He found her endearing. "There's time enough for the other stuff later. I want you well."

She took a breath as she turned her face up to him. "I'm well."

"Weller, then," he amended. "Oh, I almost forgot. I have another 'wedding present' for you."

She glanced around, expecting to see something tangible. "What is it?"

He loved the way her eyes lit up like that. It made him think of the little girl she must have once been, anticipating Christmas or her birthday. Livia, he'd heard, had been a great one for showmanship as long as there was a photographer around.

"You know how I had to keep tabs on not just you but the rest of your family, in case Livia reached out to one of you?" he asked.

Leonor nodded. "Yes?"

He knew this would make her happy. She'd lost track of one of her younger brothers and that had worried her a great deal. "Well, I found River."

Her eyes widened and she asked excitedly, "He's alive?"

"He's alive," Josh confirmed. "Turns out he was injured in the line of duty—"

She immediately thought the worst. "How serious was it?"

Josh hadn't wanted to give her too many details yet, but since she'd asked, he couldn't very well ignore her question or lie to her. But he could soften the information a little.

"Serious enough, but he definitely will survive. As a matter of fact, he's due to be discharged from the rehab facility he was sent to soon."

Leonor was overjoyed at the news. "This has to be the best medicine ever," she told Josh.

Reaching out, she touched his face and ran her hand along his cheek. This one piece of information, this one effort on his part to find out what had happened to her brother—as well as his decision to remain in Austin because this was where her life was and because it was close to her family—told her that she had really, really lucked out. She'd found someone who knew just what was important to her.

This was a man she knew she could spend the rest of her life with.

"I love you," she whispered just before she leaned in and pressed her lips against his.

After a moment, Josh drew his head back. When she looked at him quizzically, he asked, "Are you sure you're up to this?"

"I'm sure that if I have to wait any longer, I'm liable to go up in smoke."

"Certainly can't have that. Oh, and I love you, too," he told her teasingly.

"Glad we got that out of the way," she murmured against his mouth.

There was no more talking—about anything—for a long while.

* * * * *

If you loved this novel,
don't miss the next electrifying romance in
the COLTONS OF SHADOW CREEK *series:*
PREGNANT BY THE COLTON COWBOY
by Lara Lacombe,
available in May 2017
from Mills & Boon Romantic Suspense!

And check out these suspenseful titles in
USA TODAY bestselling author Marie Ferrarella's
CAVANAUGH JUSTICE *series:*

CAVANAUGH IN THE ROUGH
CAVANAUGH COLD CASE
CAVANAUGH OR DEATH
HOW TO SEDUCE A CAVANAUGH
CAVANAUGH FORTUNE

Available now from Mills & Boon Romantic Suspense!

0417/46